Realities and Alternatives

Ethan Goffman

Cyberwit.net
HIG 45 Kaushambi Kunj, Kalindipuram
Allahabad - 211011 (U.P.) India
http://www.cyberwit.net
Tel: +(91) 9415091004
E-mail: info@cyberwit.net

Printed at Replika Press Pvt. Ltd.

To Marianne

and special thanks to Karen Eilenberg

Acknowledgements

The author gratefully acknowledges the following journals for publishing versions of these stories

Raw Art Review – "Eternity"

Setu – "I'm My Own Author" and "The Realm of Wake and the Realm of Sleep"

Voices from the Fire – "One Man's Trash"

Dillinger is an artist/photographer from the Western side of Michigan. Influenced throughout the years by pop culture. Radio, TV, Movies, Comic Books, Music and Video Games. Father to 6 rad kids. Husband to an amazing Space Wife. He thrives on creativity and wants to share it with the world. Always for hire.

Mr.punkydillinger@gmail.com

Contents

Realities

The Loneliest Monk

One day Mick's family moved farther from home than Mick had known it was possible to be. He didn't want to go, but that was the way it was. His father had left for a new job a week or perhaps a month earlier—it seemed like forever—but at least Mick got to sit in front during the long car trip to their new home. They did get to stay at a Holiday Inn, but otherwise the trip took forever—there was a lot of forever going around—and he had long since given up scanning license plates, counting cars of different makes, peering out the dusty window for various kinds of animals, and other cataloging exercises. He was half asleep when his mother left him—for just a moment, she said—alone at a roadside stop. They were near their destination, but she couldn't wait.

A few people loitered. Mick stared at the dispenser machines with their rows of items he couldn't buy—cigarettes, a key chain, a nail-trimmer, a deck of playing cards. Mick wished he had someone to play cards with. He felt all alone. What was taking so long? He wandered over to a bench and sat down. Waiting, he closed his eyes. Words drifted from the next bench. Animated words. A man was talking about music. Mick opened his eyes again and glanced over. The man's voice rose as he orated to a younger woman dressed in pink who nodded in response. Mick wasn't sure, but he thought they were talking about the loneliest monk. And Mick wondered who he was, this lonely monk. Weren't all monks lonely? They had nothing to do but hang around in black robes and think about God all day. Mick knew he'd be bored if he did that. The man at the next bench certainly seemed excited about the loneliest monk. He said the monk's music was newer and more wonderful and exciting than music had ever been. And Mick imagined this lonely monk, all alone in a big field, playing sad music on a wooden flute.

Mick wasn't happy about going to a new school. He didn't know a soul. The school was at the edge of town, and everyone seemed a little bigger and a little louder than in his old school. He did make a friend the first day, a large and quiet boy named Bob. They spent all recess catching grasshoppers in the tall grass behind the school. The teacher had warned them not to stray, but soon they found themselves far away, on the edge of a woods from which the school was barely visible, atop a hill. They worked as a team, Mick driving the vaulting creatures into Bob's waiting arms. Bob would play with them for a while, then pull their legs off. Mick begged him instead to let the insects go. He had a reason for this. He had a red magic marker, and he wanted to mark the grasshoppers and see if he could catch them again later. But if Bob pulled off their legs they would just sit there and die.

There was a boy in the class, Paul Caravel, and at first Mick was happy when the teacher, reading the attendance list, called out his name. Mick liked this name. Paul Caravel. Mick kept turning it over in his mind. Paul Caravel. It sounded like a brand of ice cream or a chocolate bar. But, after a few days, Paul Caravel became Mick's worst enemy. He kept his pockets loaded with rubber bands and, when the teacher wasn't looking, would shoot them at the back of Mick's head. But, the next day, the teacher was looking. "Paul Caravel," she said in a big, disappointed voice, "I'm surprised at you. You should know better." And she marched up and made him turn over the rubber bands, although he relinquished only a couple. Mick was happy until he got stung that afternoon. The rubber band zinged off, too far for Mick to retrieve. Paul Caravel must have had more hidden.

At home Mick complained that he hated school but refused to tell his mother why. At school things grew worse. The stream of rubber bands continued, augmented by an occasional paper wad. Mick tried to fire back, but Paul always seemed to have more rubber bands, to aim better. And Mick, who sat in front, got caught by the teacher and yelled at. Soon, at recess, other kids began to fire rubber bands at Mick. And not just rubber bands, but paper wads and spitballs. Twice, the teacher caught them, but her severe warnings only deterred them briefly. One day Bob joined in the fusillade and, after that, refused to talk to Mick.

In his hometown, Mick had loved to go to the park, to fly kites, to play soccer, but now he had no one to do these things with. So he just stayed home and watched television. But he couldn't even do that, for his mother had a rule—no more than one hour of TV per day, and when she caught him trying to watch an extra episode of "Gilligan's Island," she marched him out of the house, where he played beneath the lone tree in their small back yard, digging with his plastic shovel, imagining that he had killed Paul Caravel and was burying the corpse.

The rest of the evenings, Mick just sat in his room. Now he knew why those men in the restaurant had been talking about the loneliest monk. It had been a warning. They were talking about him. But if he were a monk he had to think about God, and he didn't want to do that. His parents rarely attended church and he wasn't even sure what God was.

His mother grew worried. She asked what was the matter, why he had lost his energy and seemed so sad. Did he want to go to the park, or to take an exercise class, or to play cards? But all he wanted was to learn how to play a flute. A wooden one, if there were such things. "I think there are," said his mother. "But why are you suddenly interested in music?"

"I just am." He didn't want to tell her his reason. The loneliest monk played a wooden flute. And he was now a lonely monk. So what choice did he have? He was so insistent that the next day his mother enrolled him in lessons. From that day on, while his classmates played at recess, Mick would wonder off alone behind the little woods, across the little glen, adjacent to the bigger, deeper woods but never into them, to the smooth stones beside the brook and practice his wooden flute. At first, he just played "Twinkle Twinkle Little Star," and "Mary had a

Little Lamb," but after a few weeks he decided this wasn't good enough. Not if he wanted to be a lonely monk. He knew that lonely monks played music like nobody else. So he played in a tone as sweet and pure as he could, soft at first, then increasingly frenetic.

"Dear me, Mick," said his flute teacher. "That's interesting but you have to play the notes on the page." But Mick didn't want to play those notes. He wanted to play like the lonely monk. So he made a decision. For his teacher, he would play the notes on the page, but alone at home, or on the playground beneath the clear blue sky, he would play his own way, play whatever combination of notes leapt into his mind, furiously calling to the heavens.

One day the teacher was mysteriously absent from the playground. Paul Caravel and three other boys began to fire rubber bands at Mick. Then pebbles and stones. Mick ran to the playground's edge, but the gang of boys followed, picking up several new members in the process. "Leave me alone," shouted Mick, but Paul Caravel grabbed him. "Hey," he shouted as Mick struggled to break free, "Let's all take turns rapping him on the head." So Bob came over and, glowering above with fierce, small eyes, rapped the first rap. "Let's take his flute," said Paul Caravel, choking Mick by the windpipe. "Let's break it."

Suddenly two guardian angels swept down from the tall grasses, yelling and pushing the mob of children, who scattered like leaves in a fierce wind. What was this? Had all of Mick's flute playing reached God?

"Quick, come with us," ordered one of the guardian figures, a young woman staring, with pale green eyes, down at Mick. Each held one arm and off he ran with them. Was he running on his own? Was he dragged? Was he flying through the air? On they ran, through the thickening woods, breathlessly and without end, uphill and higher still. Pebbles got into Mick's shoes, his knee smashed into a tree branch and felt out of joint, and he wanted to stop but they wouldn't. He was gasping and if he missed school he would be in big trouble. But the taller of the two girls had a strong grip on him and if she had scared away the toughest kids in his class, Mick certainly wasn't going to fight her.

They pressed into the thickest part of the woods, the highest hill, and arrived at a dark opening, littered with stones, that plunged into the ground. "Come on," said the tall girl. "We've made a clubhouse." But Mick just stood shaking. "It's all right," said the shorter, skinnier girl, the one with green eyes. "We've gone in here dozens of times. It's safe." And she took Mick by the hand and led him in.

The girls had to stoop, but Mick's head barely brushed the cave's ceiling. Only a few twinkles of sun penetrated the darkness, but even these were lost in the thickening darkness, which continued into unknown depths.

Suddenly a yellow beam pierced the blackness. "I'm Sarah," said the taller girl, wielding a flashlight. "This is Leah."

"What's your name?" asked Leah.

"Mick."

"Oh. Well look around. We've made a secret club. See, here's our stockpile." Mick stooped and examined, while Sarah held the light. Two old candles, partly melted, the cracked skull of some animal, a tattered fan with Chinese characters, a broken pot, an old copy of Reader's Digest.

Leah crouched on the floor, lighting the candles. "The caves keep going," said Sarah.

"We go exploring," said Leah.

"But we brought you here for a reason," said Sarah.

"Yah," said Leah. "We saw all those kids picking on you and we wanted to protect you."

"But there's another reason."

"We want a cherub. We saw you practicing your flute and you looked so cute we had to steal you away to play music for us. We think you'd make a perfect cherub. And we need a cherub. We want to find love."

"Do you think you can help us find love?"

"I don't know," said Mick. "Aren't I too young?"

"Cherubs have to be young," said Leah. "Innocent. That's what makes them cherubs."

"Where are you from?" said Mick. "Shouldn't you be in school?"

"We gave up school," said Sarah. "Too boring."

"Cherubs shouldn't ask questions," said Leah. "Cherubs should just play music and be glad."

"All right," said Mick, and he got out his wooden flute and began to play Twinkle, Twinkle Little Star.

"How boring," said Leah. "Can't you play something else?"

"Anything?"

"Do you know Twinkle, Twinkle Little Bat?"

"What?"

"Twinkle, Twinkle Little Bat. It's from Lewis Carroll. Only I've never heard the music, I've just read the words. To hear the music, that would be really something!"

"Sorry," said Mick.

"What about music from Pan?"

"Who?"

"Pan. The god of revelry. Half human half goat."

"Sounds terrible," said Mick.

"I bet it would be wonderful. I bet it would."

"Oh don't mind her," said Sarah. "She's just weird."

"I don't know Pan's music either."

"Well, what do you know?" Sarah demanded.

"I know lonely monk music."

"What?"

"Lonely monk music."

"What's that?"

"That's music played only by monks in far away places. They play it and think about God."

"I don't believe in God," said Sarah.

"I do," said Leah. "But not all this Jesus stuff. I believe in the old gods, gods of woods, gods of rivers. That sort of stuff. I'm sure this cave has a god. Once I was here alone and I went exploring through a whole dark series of caves, all the way to the back. It was pitch black, and my flashlight kept flickering. I'm sure I felt him. The god of the caves."

"Were you scared?" asked Mick.

"Terrified. I ran and ran. I hit my head on a rock and it stung. My head felt wet and sticky, and my hand was covered with blood. I'm lucky I didn't fall unconscious, or I would be dead right now. Killed by the god of the caves. Finally, I reached the outdoors and I just lay there thanking the gods of sunlight that I was all right. And I didn't return to the caves for three weeks. That was the first time I showed them to Sarah."

"How long have you known about the caves?"

"Just since this summer. That was when I moved to town."

"I'm bored," said Sarah. "I've heard all this." She glared at Mick. "Aren't you going to play the flute?"

"All right. You want to hear lonely monk music?"

"Sure," said Leah. "Only I don't want you to think about God while you're playing. I want you to think about the gods."

"That's fine," said Mick. "I never used to think about God, but lately I have. But I guess if you're just listening you don't have to think about God."

So Mick began to play, and the notes echoed off the cave wall.

"That doesn't sound right," said Mick. "Let's go outside."

"Fine," said Sarah and Leah in unison. They clambered up and the sunshine blazed into Mick's eyes.

"Play now."

So Mick began again. At first everything sounded choked up like a bunch of notes that didn't really know each other. Then a bird hooted in the distance, and a woodpecker began to peck. The music sounded better, but still not right. Mick didn't know how he wanted to sound. He played a squealing sequence of notes then just gave up.

"That sounded good," said Leah.

"I don't think so. I sound much better when I'm alone. Anyway, I'd better be going. I'm much too late for school."

"School!" said Sarah. "Are you kidding? Skip it."

"I'll get in trouble."

"All right," said Leah. "We'll walk you back. Only we'd better let you off at the edge of the playground."

Not much happened on the way back, except that Leah sang twinkle twinkle little bat, but kept substituting new creatures: twinkle twinkle little cow, twinkle twinkle little walrus, twinkle twinkle little elephant, twinkle twinkle little great blue whale, twinkle twinkle little bacteria, and so on. She wanted Sarah and Mick to join in, which they did at first, but then Sarah said that it was stupid and Mick stopped singing, too. Finally, they reached the edge of the playground and Sarah shushed Leah so that they wouldn't be overheard and caught.

Class was just ending when Mick returned, and he was surprised that the teacher didn't yell at him. "Where were you?" she asked. "We were all so worried."

"I got lost in the woods."

"That's all right. But don't let it happen again. No more straying off the playground."

For the next week or so the teacher kept a sharp eye on Mick, and his classmates were chastened and subdued. Then one recess he heard a whistling from the woods, an out-of-tune version of Twinkle Twinkle . . . –and Mick snuck away and found Leah and Sarah. But they stayed near the playground and were sure to get him back quickly. This happened a few times over several weeks. There was a little stream in which water would trickle only after a rainfall and they would walk along its bed. To Mick, Leah and Sarah were goddesses who could carry him like a toy, who held and protected him in their strong arms, or else who tickled him mercilessly. Except that Leah would always have mercy and tell Sarah to stop. Then Mick would play songs on his flute: "Puff the Magic Dragon" or "This Land is Your Land" or "Swing Low Sweet Chariot." Then Leah would ask for lonely monk music, and Mick would perform different versions, after which Leah and Sarah would clap and whistle.

And then Leah would tell a story. Some of them came from books, tales of fairies and pirates and such, and some had happened to her. She talked about her older brother who used to launch war against her, throwing her about like Sarah threw Mick. Often, she would be left bruised and crying.

"I wish I had an older brother," said Mick.

Finally her brother, tired of these little wars, had joined the army and fought in a real war. He had been killed in Vietnam.

In school, and on the playground, the kids now left Mick alone. Bob even started to go hunting for bugs with him again, or they'd watch the ants, which swarmed between the rocks. Upon investigation they proved very orderly, streaming busily between various destinations. To keep things interesting, Bob and Mick would dig a trench or place stones in the ants' path, and watch the creatures reroute their journeys. Soon Bob wanted to use lighter fluid. Mick objected, because it would be hard for the ants to reroute their path if they were burning up. It turned out, though, that Bob did not have lighter fluid, so he could never carry out his plan.

One day Mick snuck off with Sarah and Leah and they ambled further than usual, from the edge of the woods to where the trees grew thick and dark—although not quite to the cave, which they had only visited that one time. Leah told a story of when she had run away from home, hitchhiking through the hot summer countryside. She had been too stupid to bring water and was lying, dehydrated and dizzy, by the side of the road with very few cars passing. Finally, a guy in a pickup truck stopped. He gave her water from a thermos, and she thanked him. The truck bumped along. Then he asked her if she had had love. He told her he could give her some good love. She said no, she didn't want any. He asked if she was sure. She said yes, so he just nodded and drove her home. He left his phone number with her, though, in case she changed her mind. She hadn't yet, but she might some day.

Then Sarah and Leah began to quarrel. Leah wanted to go to the cave, but Sarah said it was too far. Mick agreed, since he had to make it back to school. Then Leah began to pout, saying that Sarah always got her way. They fought over what Mick should play on his flute. Sarah demanded real songs, while Leah asked for lonely monk music. "That's not real music," said Sarah, and Leah answered that "at least it's not music for dull squareheads." Then Sarah called Leah a nerd and a twit and Leah called Sarah a bitch. The three of them split up, and Mick headed back to school, dejected. At the end of class that day he felt a sting at the back of his neck. Paul Caravel had struck again.

The next day it stormed but, surprisingly, Sarah and Leah showed up again. Under gray skies Mick snuck off with them, planning to stay away. If Leah and Sarah could skip school, why couldn't he? They went wading through a creek swelled with turbulent waters. Afterward, the girls took turns grabbing Mick by the hands and swinging him around. Sarah was strong and could spin him three times, but Leah could manage only once. Leah said that she should get twice as many turns because even then she wouldn't get in as many swings. Sarah said she couldn't help if Leah was a weakling and Leah said Mick should decide and Mick said he thought maybe they shouldn't swing him at all.

"See what you've done," said Sarah to Leah. "You've ruined everything."

"You're the troublemaker," said Leah, and she grabbed Mick and cradled him in her arms.

"He's mine," said Sarah. "You just let him go. You let him be with me."

"No, he's mine," said Leah, stroking Mick's hair. "He prefers me don't you Mick?"

"Bitch," said Sarah. "You called me that, but you're the bitch." And she gave Leah a rough push, but Leah held on to Mick. Then she slapped Leah in the face and Leah started slapping back. They were hitting and kicking and Mick squirmed away. Sarah knocked Leah into the mud and was on top of her pulling her hair and Leah was biting back. Stop It Mick wanted to scream, but somehow he couldn't. Sarah held down Leah's face and pushed it into the muck, twisting her arm behind her back. "Stop it," Leah said, sobbing and spattered with mud. "Stop it. I give up." But Sarah kept twisting and pushing. Finally she rose up and loomed over Leah, who lay huddled facedown and red, sobbing huge choking sobs. All three were drenched with mud, and Leah had blood mixed in, and Mick and Sarah just stood there. "Come on," Sarah finally said. "She'll be all right. Let me take you back to school."

For two weeks, Mick saw neither Leah nor Sarah. Paul Caravel disappeared, too, out of school with the chicken pox. When he returned, he seemed pale and chastened.

Mick began to wonder if Leah and Sarah were gone for good. Finally, one recess he heard Leah's strained voice calling from a distance. As Mick crossed the clump of trees, her face appeared. "Meet me at the cave as soon as class ends." Then she was gone.

Mick knew he should go home after class or his parents would worry. But he couldn't ignore Leah's message. As soon as class ended, he snuck into the woods. Only he wasn't sure where to go. He knew the cave was up a hill, but you had to go down before you went up again, and how did he know where to start going up? The trees seemed especially dense and the air was sticky. Mick felt groggy. The landscape seemed strange; even the plants looked unlike any he'd ever seen. Purple flowers appeared in intermittent patches, while odd bushes with tiny red berries grew abundantly, but Mick didn't dare touch them because they might be poison. He kept wandering, getting more and more lost.

Finally he came upon a cave. But was it the right one? And would Leah still be waiting? Nevertheless, he had to try. He stepped over the chiseled rock that guarded the entrance.

Inside it was cold and empty. He knelt and crept around searching for Leah's treasures, but they weren't to be found. Mick didn't dare explore further. But what if Leah was back there, in the darkness. An idea came; he would play his flute and, if Leah were near, it would summon her.

Mick started with a few timid notes. Then he tried "Twinkle Twinkle Little Bat." When this failed he blew louder. Finally, he was squealing with all his might, a wild cacophony of notes bleating into the darkness, echoing back or escaping the cave entrance, lost in the surrounding sky. The notes leapt out like lost little bats themselves, cascading, calling to Leah, to the surrounding wildness, to the god of the caves, to whatever forces might be out there, summoning.

From the depths something sprang out. A dark, hissing shape. A large animal? Shot through with fear, Mick scrambled ferociously out, ran wildly, pulse pounding lungs gasping feet pumping over the rocks that guarded the cave entrance into the trees through the thickening dusk.

Where was he? He was lost, his skin shivering with fear. He stood hugging a tree, heaving great breathes. The last traces of sunlight filtered through. Mick knew the sun set in the east and the school was east, so he had better follow the sunset. He walked and walked some more until he heard a shout. "Mick, is that you?" It was Leah.

She ran up to him. "Mick darling, thank God you're here. Are you lost? Come here my darling."

She cradled him in her arms, cuddled tight and warm. Her flesh felt warm and alive.

"Let's kiss," she said, pressing her lips to his, but Mick snapped his head away.

"Oh God. Everything's gone wrong. You're too young. Why does everything turn out so bad? Why am I such an idiot?"

Mick just crouched there shaking. They huddled loosely in each other's arms as the sky crept into darkness.

Next day, Mick realized he had lost his wooden flute. He was scared to tell his mother but, after a few days, she realized that he wasn't practicing. When she asked why, he confessed that he had lost the flute. Instead of getting mad, she got him a new, more expensive instrument. Somehow, though, the new flute didn't seem so interesting. He didn't want to be a lonely monk anymore, didn't want to be or do anything. At night, falling into sleep, he thought of Leah.

Mick didn't see Leah or Sarah the rest of the year, or ever again. At school occasionally someone would yell a taunt or hit him with a rubber band, but nothing worse would happen. Generally, he was ignored.

Then at recess they began to play soccer, a game Mick loved and joined in every day. Always, he played defense, scrambling and kicking at the ball, never giving up. He was proud of the goals he prevented, although the other kids didn't seem to notice. One day, with his team behind three to one, he noticed something. Paul Caravel, his teammate that day, kept getting past all the defenders except one, but somehow could never score. So Mick charged down the field to position himself beside Paul Caravel, who gave a quick kick sideways. With no one in his way, Mick scored an easy goal.

Paul Caravel scored the next goal, but was stopped from scoring after that. So Mick abandoned his position twice more and, miraculously, scored both times. Then recess ended and Mick's team had won. They gathered around him, shouting and cheering. He was a hero!

After school, when Mick was supposed to have his flute lesson, he snuck out instead, smuggling his flute and a soccer ball. Clutching the ball madly, he ran through the woods, just like he had run a few weeks before. Finally, he reached an empty parking lot up against a barren warehouse. He grabbed the flute from beneath his shirt and threw it onto the cement. It didn't break, so he kicked it away, away, into the lost woods.

He cradled the soccer ball in his arms, just as Leah had cradled him. Then he placed it down, hesitated a moment, and gave a wild, thrashing kick. He missed the solid part of the ball, the center of its energy, and it skidded away. He ran toward it, kicking madly, with more force to each kick, kicking it against the wall, great wild flailing kicks. The ball was something wild, uncontrollable, bouncing lopsidedly against the wall, against his legs and chest, skidding against the cement landscape.

He lay down on the cement, breathing heavily. He imagined a car coming from nowhere, crushing him against the cement like Bob had crushed the insects. But no car came, there was only emptiness. He rose and attacked the ball again, with increased discipline, smooth kicks toward the ball's very heart. It responded clean and smooth. He practiced dribbling it around the parking lot, kicking it hard against the wall.

The sun was sinking. Still he kicked on, panting and gasping, kicking now in angry little hops. His mind was all on the ball. He felt in savage harmony with it: ball, sphere, center of his world. The god of the ball. Leah had been right about gods, but it wasn't the god of the cave or the god of the river or the god of the sky that mattered. It was the god of the ball. Lonely monks were crazy, thinking about some God that didn't exist. And Mick kicked at the ball, weak, now, tired, again and again at the center of the sphere.

Sally, Yid Bop, and the Search for the Perfect Bird

Sally would sometimes get in trouble for drawing in class, but not as often as George. This was not because he was worse at hiding his artwork; the opposite was true. George got caught more often because he drew constantly, while Sally drew only occasionally. Nevertheless, when she did sneak a sketch, she invariably got caught. It was only years later that she was told of her unconscious habit of humming whenever she drew. "What's wrong, Sally?" the teacher would ask, and Sally never knew what had clued the teacher in. Upon investigation, the drawing would be discovered, and "Dear me, Sally," the teacher would say, "how do you expect to learn anything when you're drawing? You must pay attention. You're usually so responsible."

George was the irresponsible one. He drew always. Yet he was craftier than Sally. To avoid the teacher's eagle gaze, he sat at the rear of the class, in the far left corner. Although wanting to sit near George, Sally tended toward the middle.

Sally had only a few colored pencils, red and orange and green, which she kept concealed in her blouse pocket. George had a whole spectrum, from one edge of the rainbow to the other, as well as the gold and silver found only at the end. Most of these he kept in his lunch-pail, sneaking only a few to class to hide in the dark space beneath his desk, just the ones he wanted to use that day, so if he got caught only a few would be confiscated. Usually, the teacher was forgiving and would return the pencils after class. "George Levine," she would say, although she rarely sounded angry, "how are you ever going to learn anything if you just sit there drawing?"She did seem to like his drawings, though. But then everyone liked his drawings; Sally wished she could draw like him. His figures seemed to pop from the page, writhing with movement.

Sally's, by contrast, appeared flat and lifeless. And he drew so many things. Sometimes, like most of the children, he drew flowers, houses, and people, but more often he constructed strange creatures. Early in the year he concentrated on dragons—large beastly ones with flaming eyes, small ornamental ones along the edges of pages, elongated Chinese ones with wrinkled foreheads, and a monstrous one with a huge, bushy mustache that looked just like Groucho Marx (if he had happened to be a dragon). Then, for a while, George seemed bored with mythical creatures and drew horses, camels, and elephants, with astonishing realism. When fantastical creatures returned, however, they grew quickly stranger, passing through a brief gorgon phase to various mixtures and mutants. There was a red and brown monster like a boiling pool of lava, with tentacles spewing every which way and two heads (with three eyes each, including a big middle one for tracking creatures flying overhead). The first head was locked in battle with a naked, hairy ogre, while the second devoured a maiden. She was already swallowed from the waist up, and only her billowing dress and two kicking legs remained sticking from its mouth. In the distance, alone in a corner, a single knight galloped to save her. But he was too late.

Sally vaguely wished she could draw like this, but had no idea how to get started. Still she was content enough drawing one thing: birds. One bird followed by another bird. Small and off-center, they never filled the page. They didn't really resemble birds so much as crooked, bloated creatures with tiny wings that should never have been able to carry them aloft. And in such drab colors. Sally wished that she had more colored pencils, but somehow never thought of asking her parents to buy them.

But she persevered, for she had a goal. Once, in a picture book perhaps, or perhaps at a zoo, she had seen a wonderful bird. She wasn't sure of the color. Was it pink? She had been very young. Was it a peacock or a flamingo? Surely not a common robin, but who knew? Still, she kept this unknown bird in her mind. This was why she kept up with her scribblings. And throughout that year, if intermittently, she continued in her quest to draw the perfect bird.

***

Seven years later, Sally sat cross-legged on the floor of a used-book store, searching through *Barnham's Big Book of Birds*, staring at a brown and red Turkey-Eagle, who looked more like a turkey than an eagle, and who stared back with curious young eyes.

"Still interested in birds?" A voice floated from above. She glanced up to round glasses and stringy red hair that she hadn't seen in a long, long time. It was George.

What are you doing in town?" she asked.

"Just visiting. And you?"

"I'm only browsing. I come in this shop a lot."

"It's a nice store. If we hadn't moved, I'd be in here all the time, too."

A pause. Sally didn't know what to say, so she flipped the page.

"That's an interesting bird." George pointed from above. "What is it, some kind of flamingo?"

"Which one, this?" She pointed at a pink-winged creature with a neck curved to form an S. "It says it's a Greater Flamingo."

"Greater than what?"

"I don't know. I don't care about names, I just like to look at the pictures."

"Do you still like to draw birds? Are you looking for models to copy?"

"Oh, I never draw nowadays. Well, not very often. I'm just curious—I'm looking for a certain kind of bird."

"What kind?"

"I'm not really sure."

"Then how will you know when you find it?

"I'll just know."

"Mmm," said George. He loomed overhead for a moment, prepared to leave, hesitated, then withdrew. Sally leafed through the book. A robin, ho hum. Ho dee hee. Still the book did need to include all creatures. But wait, a Scarlet Cock of the Rock glared from beneath its crimson plume. And a Crowned Crane and a Blue Gallinule. Randomly, she flipped, landing upon a Great Horned Owl which crouched in a feathered mass upon a tree-limb, its triangular ears and triangular mouth forming a greater triangle, an almost perfect shape. Its eyes were supposed to symbolize wisdom. She peered at them, they peered back. She knew she could never beat it in a staring contest. She wasn't sure if the eyes held wisdom, but deep within the irises she thought she saw something. . . .

A shadow fell upon the book, preceding a voice, just as lightening precedes thunder. Thankfully, the voice was much kinder than thunder. "Listen," it said tentatively. "Wanna go somewhere for coffee?" It was George.

"All right."

Outside, the December wind whipped through her garments, which Sally pulled tightly about herself. They had, she thought, a choice. "Do you want to go to Buffalo Bills or to the Java Joint?"

Walking in rhythm—ta tap ta tap ta tooey—talking about life since George had moved away, Sally asked most of the questions. At first, he was reluctant to talk, but gradually his tongue loosened. Yes, he enjoyed high school, at least some of the time, but no, he wasn't looking forward to returning now that break was ending. Did he still draw those fantastic creatures? Yes, but not in class any more. Except in art class, of course. And had he enjoyed the holidays? Yes and no. He had spent Hanukkah at home surrounded by relatives from New York—"a bunch of stodgy Wall Street types, who only care about stocks and bonds." His brother-in-law, who just a year ago had made his first million, had lost most of it through his investments in a small computer company gone sour. George liked that; he thought it much more interesting when people lost great sums of money than when they gained them. He most enjoyed his great uncle Karl, who told tales of when he had fought for the anarchists in the Spanish Civil War and who, while wounded in the thigh in a hospital bed, had actually met Ernest Hemingway. Still, he wondered why the family even got together to celebrate Hanukah when they didn't do anything else Jewish.

After all this talk, Sally didn't know what to say. She wished he would ask about her, but he didn't. But then again, what did she have to say? George was so much more interesting. They walked on—ta tap ta tap ta tooey—and she remained silent and he remained silent. She grew distracted. Instead of watching him, or the gray pavement ahead, she watched the sky, which was round and blue today, although broken by a few furious wisps of clouds, and across which a single bird, a blank bird, an any-kind-of-bird, thrust itself on its own wings on a flight of its own making.

Suddenly George spoke. "What are you humming?"

"Oh, am I humming? Oh yes I am. I'm humming 'It's Too Darn Hot.' What a strange song to pick. I don't even like Frank Sinatra. And what a strange day to be humming."

I like that," said George. "Humming 'It's Too Darn Hot' in freezing weather."

"Uh huh," said Sally, and she continued humming, but more self-consciously now.

"You know what your humming needs?"

"What?"

"More zest. More life. More energy."

"Why? I'm just humming."

"You're not <u>just</u> humming. You shouldn't *just* do anything. You have to put energy into everything you do."

"But what can you do with humming except to hum?"

"Do a skat version. Like this: dah doo wee dobbah, wee dobbah dee doo. Like Ella Fitzgerald."

"I'm afraid I don't listen to her."

"Not too many people do these days. I guess I'm just old fashioned."

"Besides it's silly. People will laugh. And you can't even carry a tune."

"That's not important. All that matters is how much spirit you put into it. Music should be hot, to melt the snow. You have to improvise."

"But I'm not the improvisational type."

"Now's the time to learn. Listen: Dah dooh dah dee doh, da woopah dee bop."

"It doesn't even sound like music. I'm sure Ella Fitzgerald doesn't sound like that."

"It's a new form of music. It's Jewish bop music."

"I don't think so."

"It's Yid Bop."

"Yid Bop?"

"Jewish Jazz. Listen. A bupp a doowop, buh dooh bidee dooh. Now you try it."

"No."

"Why not?"

"Because . . . well, it's Jewish music and I'm not really Jewish. I'm only half Jewish."

"Half is good enough."

"But it's my father. It's the wrong half."

"Mother, father, who cares? Just some old religious laws."

"But I never go to synagogue or anything."

"So, neither do I. That's not what makes you Jewish."

"So what does?."

"Don't worry about it. You're Jewish enough. Quit arguing and just sing."

"No. Leave me alone."

At this rebuff, George gave up. And they walked on in silence: trudge, trudge, trudge. On the curb the last remnants of Monday's snowfall had turned into a brown mush. The brown buildings of Evanston stretched out, all suddenly alike, in every direction. Sally realized that they were not headed toward a specific coffee shop, but wandering aimlessly. She gazed up at an empty grayish sky devoid of birds, devoid of clouds and airplanes. A complete emptiness, a round and pure emptiness, a blank slate. Even the coldness seemed somehow pure, somehow renewing. And on they walked—trudge, trudge, trudge— silent. And out of nowhere a spark struck in Sally's mind. Not quite fire, but a spark.

"Ta de ta."

"Huh," said George. "What was that?"

"Ta de ta. Ta de ta Do."

"Not bad," said George. "Not bad at all. But it needs more . . . more variety."

"Ta de Do de Do de Dah."

"Better. Keep it up and I'll accompany."

"Ta de ta de Dah Do."

"Dooh bopsie beeah bah beeah bah bop." From a passing mink coat stared a woman's startled face, but George paid it no mind. "Wah rahah scoobey dah boobey dee Bop."

"No, that's not right," said Sally.

"Why not?"

"We're not in unison. You're drowning me out."

"I think we're fine. Yid Bop is a syncopated, individualistic, do your own thing kinda music."

Suddenly, "Look," said George, pointing at a nearby shop window.

"What?" Sally asked. "Glasses?" The shop was filled with all variety of glasses, from black to brown to green to screaming pink, from conservative to horned to wire-rim to funky.

"That pair . . . ." He stretched his arm, pointing to the rear.

"What, those purple and red things? Are they even glasses?"

"Don't you think they'd be perfect for Yid-Bop?"

"They look ridiculous."

"Exactly. Just what we want."

"Can we even afford them?"

"I have ten dollars Hanukah money. Is that enough?"

"I have no idea. You're the one with glasses."

"But not way-out, funky, psychedelic classes."

Sally found herself following George into the store, where the proprietor had, not screaming purple, but bland oval glasses, and a bland oval face to match. He asked, "What can I do for you?" and Sally decided he had a gentle voice.

When George remained silent, Sally nudged him. "Well?"

"Oh," said George. "We're just looking."

"How much," Sally asked boldly, "for those glasses in the window?"

"Which ones?"

"Those purple things."

"You see," said George, "we've invented a new form of music, and we need a look to fit our image."

"Strange. And what might this new music be?"

"We call it Yid Bop."

"Yid Bop?"

"It's the smashingest music around. It's taking the country by storm."

"So what's the price?" asked Sally.

"For you," said the salesman, "I'm willing to offer a special price. A ten percent discount, since it's for a good cause. Only eighteen dollars and fifty cents."

"Eighteen fifty," George exclaimed. "We can't afford that. We're poor Jews from the outer city. We can't afford that."

"I'm sorry, kids, but that's the best I can offer."

"Well let's look around a bit . . . ."

Just then a real customer entered the store, rather plump and quite well dressed, and he drew the salesman to him like an electric zapper draws a bug. And it was "can I help you, sir," and "this style will suit you well." The man, Sally overheard, needed his bifocals replaced by trifocals. My, how could one set of eyes need correction in so many ways? The two droned on for awhile while Sally looked over the display case one last time to make sure they hadn't missed any bargains. "Come on," George whispered. "Let's get out of here."

Outside, the last of the snow was melting, along with the end of the winter holiday, which seemed wasted. The corner Santa was gone, replaced by a chubby man who gasped and breathed out strands of white smoke as he walked. "Aren't we going to sing Yid Bop?" Sally inquired.

"Without those glasses? I don't think so."

"We don't need glasses."

"I told you no," George grunted. "You were right before. There's nothing especially Jewish about Yid-Bop."

"Mmmm." They walked on a bit and suddenly Sally spoke up. "Why not make it more Jewish?"

"How?"

"We could add Jewish phrases. In Hebrew or Yiddish or something."

"What a great idea."

"There's just one problem. I don't know any Hebrew or Yiddish. Do you?"

"Only a couple of stodgy old prayers. But I know a few words in Yiddish."

"Let's try it."

"Oy vey is mir. Ba boy ba beer. Hmmm, this is going to be difficult."

"Schlemiel," said Sally. "That's the only Yiddish word I know. Schlemiel doo ah dooie. How does that sound?"

"Needs work."

"We need to change the melody to fit the new words."

"Make it more like prayers in a synagogue."

"Of course. Only I've never been to synagogue."

"I've only been a few times, but I think I remember how it sounds."

"With your ear for music, it won't sound right anyway."

"Oye Vey, Oy-Eeeee Vey, we are two little Jews who have lost our way."

"Oy vey, oy vey, boop de boop de boop de bey."

"Nu, Nu, we're true Jews."

"What's this 'Nu'? I've never heard that."

"It's an expression. It's . . . hard to explain."

"Oy vey, oy vey, loop de loop de loop de hey."

"Momma's little baby loves chicken soup."

"Oy vey, oy vey, scoop de scoop de scoop de dey."

"And momma's little baby loves Shiksas too."

"Hey," said Sally. "I don't appreciate that."

"Tuchus, schlong, let's sing our song."

"You're disgusting."

"Your Yiddish is better than I thought."

Just then they came upon "Ray's Records," a funny old shop that Sally rarely entered. But again she had an idea. "Why don't we look for old Jewish music. That way we can make Yid Bop even better."

The darkened shop breathed a musty smell. Empty, except for George and Sally. Even the proprietor was gone. Who would leave a shop all alone? A shop so empty that there was no danger of thievery, for no thief would bother entering.

And no CDs. This shop was definitely not cutting edge. In front were bins of ancient tapes. Sally imagined them squeaking and crackling, still trying to fling out the old songs that had once made people happy. Mostly, though, there was vinyl. Old fashioned record albums. On one side the young, unkempt members of The Who gazed at Sally and George, half rebellious, half eager to please. On the other, an older and wiser Dinah Washington peered from a tattered record cover. Rows of albums extended into a dark cave. Who knew where it ended? Was the musty spell due to the vinyl? No, that would smell all modern and plastic and squeaky clean. Perhaps it was the smell of old cardboard, but Sally thought it emanated from the rear.

From the rear there came a creaking sound. Out of the darkness, a lone figure wandered. An old man with a bit of a limp and a face creased with wrinkles that seemed to smile.

"Can I help you?"

"We're looking for Yid Bop."

"Oh, don't," said Sally. "This is getting embarrassing."

"Yid Bop? What's that?"

"Yid Bop. Jewish jazz."

"Jewish jazz? Do you mean klezmer?"

"Klezmer? What's that?"

"You don't know klezmer?"

"No."

"Young man, are you Jewish?"

"I guess so."

"You guess so? Either you are or you aren't. But tell me, by Jewish jazz do you mean jazz by Jewish musicians?"

"Is there much?"

"Is there much? What about Benny Goodman and Stan Kenton? What about Davie Brubeck. And of course George Gershwin, the father of them all. Why without the Jewish influence, the whole history of jazz would be different."

"Oh. Well. Learn something new every day."

"Obviously you have a lot to learn. Don't know your own history. Not in the old world and not in America. A lost soul."

"I'm not lost."

"Then where are you?"

"I'm right here in Evanston Illinois in the good old U.S.A."

"Am I lost?" asked George, back out on the frosty street. From his arms dangled a brown bag containing two albums recommended by the proprietor. Having just switched over to CD's, he would have to play them on his parents' old stereo.

"I like you the way you are. If you don't know something, make it up. That's better than the real history." And she squeezed his hand tightly. "Come on, one more round of Yid Bop."

"Let me listen to these old records first. Do a little research."

They trudged on and in a few blocks spotted, way down the street, a black man carrying a guitar case. "Look," whispered George, nudging over to Sally. "A musician. Let's sing some Yid Bop for him."

"You're crazy."

"Come on. Let's start now so we can get warmed up." Sally remained silent, so George started up on his own. Reluctantly, Sally joined in.

The man approached and George sang boldly into his face. Quietly, embarrassed to sing but embarrassed not to, Sally joined in.

"Wah," said the black man. "What are you saying?"

"It's Yid Bop."

"Yid what?"

"Yid Bop. It's a new form of music. It's a cool groove thing. It's sweeping the country."

"It's the 1980s. There's no more Bop of any kind. Just heavy metal and Ronald Reagan." George came to a silent halt. "Besides," said the man, "you've got to learn to sing in tune before you go approaching people on the street. If you could do that, I'd throw you a quarter. Gotta support the street musicians. Heh heh." George was silence and, as the man walked away, they heard him muttering, "Crazy kids. Crazy kids."

"He should understand," said George in a small voice. "A musician should understand." Silently they walked on two blocks, three blocks, five, and the cold numbed Sally's ears.

"Come on," she said. "Let's sing."

"What's the use."

"Don't look so dejected. What did that guy know? Get into the Yid Bop spirit."

"I've given up. I'll never sing Yid Bop again."

"Come on. Lah di lah." Silence. "Bop di bah," Sally burst out, louder than she thought she would dare. A small woman carrying two very large grocery bags stared.

"Will you shut up?" said George. "The whole Yid Bop idea was stupid."

"Sorry." They were getting nowhere. They would never reach a coffee shop, and Sally didn't even want to talk to George or be with him, but she didn't know how to say goodbye. She was only trying to help. Why did he have to be so rude?

They walked on. Ta-tap, ta-tap, ta-tap. And suddenly, out of annoyance, with vengeful purpose (yet softly out of fear) she uttered a single line. "Loopah de Doopah."

And something about this line seemed right.

Yes, Loopah de Doopah, that was it. More loudly. "Loopah de Doopah."

"Ska looah bohee da boopah di bop. Cool groove man," George joined in.

And, with more energy and harmony than before the two joined together. Sally's soft, lush voice filled the air, repeating and repeating, circling harmoniously upon itself, intermixing with George's harsher, quicker variations. Their voices blended, bouncing forward on cold winter gusts, dancing on frosty breath, together, sung out to passing pedestrians, an audience with shopping bags and briefcases. A short break in the routine. Yid Bop, the music of the day, a brief visitor traveling through on the frosty air.

***

In greens and blues, the tail spread. The bird's wings fanned out across the pale green page. It was shortly joined by other birds, of similar design although smaller and in different colors. A red and yellow one flapped just above, just behind. And below in a corner hovered a little gray one, struggling not to fall off the page. All the same pattern, stylized, with block colors and triangular wings. All faced forward, staring, with big and round and solid eyes.

Sally sat in the basement of the Sears Building, where she worked, fifty-seven flights above, as a computer programmer. She was alone at a table, beneath a sign that said "Wyoming." She was waiting for George in the American Room, which was decorated in red, white, and blue, and contained fifty pillars, each with the name of a state. Wyoming was at the back. Sally thought that the designers must have planned to put silhouettes of the states under their names, but had run out of money.

Looking up, she saw George at the distant cash register paying for his meal. He had been gone for some time now. Gone to California but still, even from a distance, he had that same ragged look, like someone who couldn't quite remember where he was. As he crossed the room, he balanced his tray precariously on one arm and she was sure it would fall. Somehow, he made it and, sitting down, asked how she was.

"Oh fine, but I've had a frantic day."

"Why?"

"There was a horrid computer glitch and no-one could locate it except me. Still my co-workers made fun of me. They said that I'm too young to save the day. I'm used to being the oldest, not the youngest."

"But you did save the day."

"Yep."

"So what was wrong?"

"Well, actually, the problem was with a program I worked on, so it could have been my fault, but it was in a section written by Jim, another programmer. Anyway, we had been getting calls complaining. For no apparent reason, a store would suddenly get, say, 18 or 21 or 127 trash baskets instead of the number they had ordered. We weren't sure if it was a computer problem the first time, because it was such an anomaly. But once it became clear that our department had something to do with it, we got on the case."

"Sounds like you have a challenging job."

"Sometimes. It can get hectic. I like the job. I almost love it. But what you do sounds so much more exciting."

"I doubt it. It's no way to earn a living."

"But you get to be on the covers of magazines and stuff. I even bought a couple of issues of *Fantasy and Science Fiction* that featured your work."

"Yeah. That's great when I get a sale. And I have some connections now. Still, it's a haphazard way to live."

"But you get to use your imagination at something you love, something you've been doing since you were a child. And all that time you spent drawing has led to a career. All that time getting chastised in the back of the room, and you were the one really getting an education."

"I guess so, but you haven't done too badly yourself. You have a real job."

"But you're an artist."

"A limited artist. I'm not even sure what that the word means. Artist? I'm no Rembrandt, that's for sure. I have a certain craftsmanship and a certain imagination, in a limited way. Actually, I was thinking about going back to school, picking up some computer graphics, going into commercial art."

"Commercial art? That's a disappointment."

"I don't see what there is to be disappointed about. But I see you still draw," he said suddenly leaning over.

"Oh, I always have time left over at lunch. And right now the schedule's staggered so that I eat alone. So I've taken up drawing again."

"Still drawing birds. Some things don't change. And they're all the same."

"This is the bird I've always been trying to draw. The idea was in my head for years, but it wouldn't come out. Finally, one day I was sick at home. Actually, I felt all right except that when I tried to walk around my stomach started churning. I had slept so much I couldn't sleep any more and television got to be a drag. I needed to *do* something. So what did I do? I drew."

"And?"

"And it just spilled out. This bird I've been thinking of my whole life."

"Mind if I try a few?"

"Go ahead. Though it's not really fair, my having to compete with a big-time artist."

"Not so big time. Pass me a yellow chalk."

"Careful. They smudge your hands."

"I know that."

"Oh yes. Of course."

George's first bird resembled Sally's, but with a longer, curved beak, and glaring eyes.

And he drew a small yellow one, diving with wide-open wings, plunging down the page. He drew with shadow and depth, from different angles: straight ahead, in profile, soaring away in the distance, plummeting in search of prey. They turned and twisted, fluttering around and between Sally's birds, graceful forms flying between set forms, intertwining against the pale green paper sky.

Secretly, however, Sally preferred hers. All neat and orderly. Such clear bright colors. It was the best design. It was the perfect bird.

Lucy Comes Back

Once, there were five college students who lived in an off-white house at the edge of the Earlham College campus. They were all quite young and carefree except for Renaldo, the youngest of them all, who was a bit of a worry to the others.

One quiet October morning, Renaldo lounged on the front porch, studying. Brown leaves covered the lawn, rustling only slightly. On the trees the leaves, having abandoned the year's greenness, splashed a bright deluge—orange, red, purple—and Renaldo, glancing up from his book, thought he noticed a single pink leaf hanging eccentrically from an oddly shaped dogwood that didn't fit in with the oaks and elms that dotted the campus and surrounding neighborhoods. Renaldo returned to reading, not Thucyides' *History of the Peloponessian War,* nor Dickens' *Bleak House,* nor *Principles of Chemistry,* but Seuz's *The Cat in the Hat Comes Back.* He had already read it six times that year, as it seemed to him the most enjoyable book in the house.

However, seven times was proving too much, as his mind and his eyes kept wandering. Through the kitchen window, he glimpsed Persephone, one of his housemates, doing dishes. From this angle, the windowsill cut off her head, which ordinarily he would have found frustrating. Ordinarily, he loved to glance at her twisting golden mane of hair, which was continually bouncing and rearranging itself into shapes of sheep, dragons, gypsies, bushbabies, fruit bats, great (and wise) horny owls, spotless leopard cubs, and creatures so obscure as not to be named. More fun than the clouds to ponder (come to think of it, didn't those fuzzy gray clouds above appear on the verge of an outburst?).

Recently, however, Persephone had decided to lop her golden locks off and dye them green, and now they were of no interest to Renaldo whatsoever. He had begged her not to cut her hair, or at least to dye it pink, for god's sake, a far nicer color than green, but she had just laughed. "Oh, Renaldo, you're such an innocent."

What was that noise? The phone ringing, but let someone else get it. Renaldo gazed at the brown leaves decaying on the lawn. The leaves were smart to escape the oncoming winter this way. Later, in warm weather, new leaves would sprout. When Renaldo died, nothing would grow from him; only worms would feed on his body. Still, worms needed to live too. What did everyone have against poor worms? They made the soil rich which, Renaldo thought, was more useful than anything he had ever done.

"Damn it, Renaldo," pronounced Marmaduke bursting through the front door. "Why don't you ever answer the phone?"

"It's never for me."

"It is today. And why do you always leave your dishes for Persephone?"

"I was getting to them."

"You're always getting to them, but never arriving."

"I thought Persephone was doing her own dishes, not mine."

"She always ends up doing your dishes."

"I have to get the phone."

Renaldo returned from the phone call with an evil smile on his face. "Guess who's visiting?"

"Oh God no," said Marmaduke. "It sounded like Lucy. She couldn't be visiting again!"

"It is," said Renaldo.

"God help us."

"What does everyone have against Lucy?"

"She's a lunatic."

"All right, so she's a lunatic. But she's a lot of fun."

"And she's even worse than you about the dishes."

***

Lucy appeared that afternoon some two hours later than expected, which for her was early. Following severe pressure from his roommates, Renaldo was doing that day's lunch dishes, and John and Betsy, Renaldo's other roommates, were the first to spot Lucy from the front porch.

"Hello kids," she intoned as she bounced on her tall, skinny legs up the steps. "I brought some pickles. Want some? Kosher."

"No thanks. Renaldo is inside doing dishes."

"On a nice day like this?"

"It's supposed to rain."

"Not yet. While it's nice, he should be outside enjoying the fall."

Lucy bounced, at her jaunty, lanky, unnatural gait, into the house and pulled Renaldo by his elbow (it was all Renaldo could do to avoid dropping a particularly disgusting, egg-stained pan). "Those yucky dishes will wait. C'mon out, the weather's fine. Wait, have a pickle—where can I leave them. Oh, someone's been baking banana cake, let me have a quick slice, I'm starved. You have a slice too. What, we don't need plates, we can eat and walk at the same time—you're smart enough to do that, aren't you?"

And out they scurried, into the wide waiting world, across the main path through campus, past the marbled arches of the main hall, past students tossing frisbees—indeed, a wicked silver frisbee somehow sliced between Lucy's rapidly pedaling legs and bonked Renaldo in the ankle—past the old cemetery at the back of campus (Lucy wanted to dance on the graves, but Renaldo worried that people would see), through a cornfield browning with dying stalks, into the lush depths of the forest tucked away behind campus where few students went (Renaldo remembered being lost back there one night, fearing snakes in the darkness).

***

A maelstrom of leaves and wind swirling about, Renaldo and Lucy galloping through the muck, trees whizzing by, branches whipping at Renaldo, flies and birds skimming by, mosquitos sucking, as Lucy and the wind pulled him along. Finally, out of breath, they paused to rest beneath an old oak. Renaldo plopped upon the ground, panting heavily. After a brief pause, "All right," said Lucy, "let's get going."

"I'm tired."

"Lazy bones. You gotta get more exercise."

"I have to study."

"Ya, right. If I studied the way you do, I'd have flunked out long ago."

"You did flunk out."

"Ya, but I'll be back some day. And when I do, watch out—straight As. I'm gonna tear this college up. And I'm not gonna use you as a role model, that's for sure."

"So when are you returning?"

"Soon, but I'm not quite ready. Come on, let's go."

Renaldo meant to protest, but Lucy was already bounding ahead through wilderness. He sprinted to catch up.

"You remind me of my old cat, Oliver," said Renaldo, "the way he bounced through the weeds behind the house."

"That's silly," said Lucy, slowing down. "I'm not nearly graceful enough."

"Oliver was probably the least graceful cat that ever lived."

"Gee, thanks."

"Well, for a human to be as graceful as the least graceful cat is still pretty good."

"Julie Yankelmeyer had cats. You remember Julie Yankelmeyer? She had two cats, Herbert and Sherbert, but she couldn't even take care of them. When they were kittens, boy, she played with them and fed them. But as they grew up, she would leave them outside. Once. she even left them out all night with the rats and the cockroaches and the cold night air. And smack, a car walloped them. Teenagers drag-racing. One car ran them down both at once, leaving two bloody streaks splattered across the road."

"That's awful!"

"I never did trust that Julie Yankelmeyer. Irresponsible, that's the only word for her. If you have cats, you should take care of them. Irresponsible."

"I guess so," said Renaldo, but there was a waver in his voice.

"But you're not like that. You take good care of Oliver."

"Ya except . . . well I kind of forgot to feed him for a few days. And he ran off and kind of fell asleep under the hood of a car."

"Was he all right."

"He was until the engine got turned on."

"Oh. That's horrible. Oh."

They walked on in silence, deeper into the woods.

"Anyway," said Lucy, "you're not like Julie Yankelmeyer. Didn't you tell me that you picked up Oliver as a stray? So he was kind of just an accident anyway, right?"

"I guess so."

"Besides, you're young. Julie Yankelmeyer should know better at her age."

"Yeah, I guess she graduated last year and I'm only a junior."

"Come on, I'll race up that hill."

"I'm tired. I want to go home."

"We've only just begun."

"It's getting cold out. And it's starting to rain."

"One little drop."

"And I'm hungry."

"Hungry. Tired. Cold. What a whiner. Look. I brought banana bread and pickles. When we reach that oak, we'll eat."

The oak wasn't very far, but banana bread doesn't go with pickles, and Lucy had only bought enough banana bread for herself, and the pickles were sour.

"Funny you should bring up Julie Yankelmeyer," said Lucy as she gobbled the last few crumbs of banana bread.

"I didn't bring her up. You did."

"Anyway, I visited her this summer up in Chicago. And she was excited because she had a boyfriend. Her first. All through college she never had a boyfriend and now she had one and she invited me up to Chicago especially to meet him. And you know what he was?'

"What?"

"A real loser. His name was Ralph and he didn't even brush his hair or tuck in his shirt, and he had bad breath like he didn't brush his teeth."

"Your shirt's not tucked in," said Renaldo. "And your hair's kind of messy."

"You too. But it's all right, cause we're old friends. But this guy was just a lazy bum. I mean, here he was meeting someone new and he couldn't even brush his hair. Plus he didn't even have a job. He was satisfied borrowing money from Julie, and he had the nerve to ask me to pay for lunch, and I'm sure I'll never see the money again. And I brought a box of those fancy chocolates, Sees, from California, and he didn't even thank me."

"He sounds lousy," said Renaldo.

"Maybe not that bad. I hope I haven't given the wrong idea. I mean, he is in school studying computers, or at least he said he was. And he did seem to care for Julie, I guess. Anyway, something happened, not with him but with a friend of his named Joe who drove us to dinner. Joe, what a basic name. I mean, when you meet a Joe, anything could happen, good or bad."

"So what happened with this Joe?"

"All through dinner that night, this Joe kept leering at me with this sly look. He even winked at me a couple of times. But what did I want with him? He was even more seedy and unkempt than Julie's boyfriend. And he kept asking questions, like about my job and my family and whether I had a boyfriend. Nosier and nosier and I didn't think it was any of his business, so I told him to buzz off. And you know what he said?"

"What?"

"'Did anyone ever tell you you're beautiful when you're angry?' God, I thought, do people really use that line. Well, the way he said it he tried to sound cocky, but there was a waver in his voice. The rest of dinner he was kind of quiet, but afterward we went to a bar where a band was playing the blues, but the instruments were out of tune and much too loud. I decided I should try to talk to this Joe, so I asked him about his job and his family. He didn't say much about either, but like Ralph he said he was studying computing and he definitely wanted to get married some day.

"Afterward, when we were ready to leave, Julie announced that she was going to her boyfriend's apartment and that Joe would take me home. She kind of smiled at Joe, like there was something in the offing. Well, I certainly didn't want to be part of a scheme with any old Joe, especially not with this one, so I said I would take a cab. Julie looked upset and said, 'Come on Lucy, why do you have to spoil everything?' But I said that there was nothing to spoil. So I stood at the side of the street and the three of them drove off saying it would take all night to get a cab, but I got one in three minutes."

Renaldo noticed that, instead of getting closer to home, they were getting deeper into the woods. He had never realized that these woods were so dense and deep. But when Lucy was telling a story it was hard to interrupt.

"Next day, what do you know, I realized I'd left my Sees chocolates. In Joe's car. Julie hadn't bothered to get them for me. So it was up to me to go to Joe's apartment to retrieve them, which is the last thing in the world I wanted to do.

"I arrived late in the evening. Joe's apartment looked like him, run down and seedy, with a veneer of cleanliness. Wet dishes, like they'd just been washed, were scattered by the sink, and magazines were piled in haphazard little stacks. To the side was a crooked pile of Schlitz six-packs. The television was blaring PBS, asking for money as usual, and Joe smelled of some disgustingly strong menthol aftershave, though somehow he didn't quite look shaved.

"He told me that he was just about to watch the McNeil Lehrer report because he found it important to keep up with world events. I said I found McNeil Lehrer the most boring show imaginable and to please hand over my chocolates. Then he tried to tell me how fascinating that I had brought fancy chocolates all the way from California, but I told him I was in a hurry and had to leave. Instead of taking the hint, he asked if I had time for dinner first and I refused. Finally, he said if I would just talk to him for fifteen minutes, he would give up the chocolates. I said ten. We negotiated to 12 ½. But first I made him get out the box of chocolates, so I could be sure he had them in hand.

"I kept careful time on my watch as he launched into a monologue about the stars, how there were hundreds of millions of them, and black holes and quasars, and how new evidence about the possibilities of non-oxygen-based life made it almost certain that life existed on other planets, and how scientists had all kinds of installations searching for life. 'Don't you think it's wonderful'? he said.

"'It sounds pretty terrible to me,' I answered.

"'How can you say that? It means that humans aren't alone, that other lifeforms could be out there building spaceships and exploring the universe, that they could have all kinds of marvelous inventions to share with us. Why, it boggles the mind!'

"'It doesn't boggle my mind.'

"'Why not?'

"'Look,' I said, 'what do you think we humans are in the universe?'

"'I don't know.'

"'Little snits. And what does it make us if there's other intelligent life?'

"'What?'

"'Even littler snits. There's five billion of us already, and I'm only one of that five billion, and if there's other forms of life that makes me even more insignificant. If I'm only one of five billion, at least I want to be part of the only intelligent species in the universe.'

"He just stood there dumbstruck.

"'Your time is long up,' I said, and headed toward the box of chocolates. But he was faster than me—he lunged in front of it. 'Don't be so mean,' he said. 'I only want to talk to you because you're beautiful and fascinating.'

"'There's nothing fascinating about you,' I said.

"At that, he grew menacing. 'You only want to mistreat me, like every other woman,' he said. 'I deserve better.' Then he grabbed me, started to kiss me as I pushed him away. 'Keep back,' I shouted, but he came at me again.

"So I grabbed one of his empty beer bottles. 'I don't have time to play games. Let me go or I'll smash you. I mean it!' I gave him my meanest look. I slapped the bottle against my hand several times. But he just stood there. It was stalemate."

A jag of lightning sliced the sky. A growl of thunder, the hiss of wind, and the rain poured down.

Renaldo and Lucy scurried through blinding blasts of water, over slippery, splattering mud. Gusts of rain flung against Renaldo's flesh as if to penetrate. A sneaky tree branch hit him in the eye. Finally, as he leapt forward over a bush, Renaldo's right foot slipped beneath him, and the rest of his body followed. He lay there panting as the rain pounded. Where was Lucy?

Time was all murky, but at some point there was a brief lull in the storm. Renaldo coughed, blew water from his nose, wiped his eyes, gazed at the dangling gray clouds arched overhead in all directions. As he rose, an ugly drizzle met him, not as heavy as the earlier storm but somehow damper. His drenched clothes dragged him, but he stumbled forward, downhill because that was the easiest direction. Luckily, he came upon a huge jutting rock leaning away from the wind. He crouched at the rock's base, which offered some protection as he awaited the storm's end.

***

An unfamiliar green-haired visage stared from the mirror across the room, startling Persephone with its oddness, till she realized that it was *her*. Persephone glanced across the couch, over her black t-shirt, to her blue-jean sheathed legs, which lay sprawled on the other side. From this position, she could scrutinize all of herself, head and body, at intriguing angles. In the distance, mumbling voices grew more distinct as full consciousness returned.

"Wash off this brush," Lucy's shrill voice pierced into the heart of the house from the front porch. "And hand me that chair. And be careful with that bucket."

"Hold on," replied Renaldo. "I can't be everywhere at once."

Persephone snuck over to the window to check out what was going on. "By the way," said Renaldo, "you never got to the end of that story."

"What story?"

"You know, about Julie Yankelmeyer and your visit to Chicago and that Joe guy."

"Oh, that story. Joe let me go—what else could he do? But I never did get those chocolates back."

"That's it? Rather anticlimactic"

"Yep, that's it."

"You didn't smash his head in or anything?"

"Why should I? I'm not a violent person."

Curiosity nipped at Persephone and she opened the front door, stepped outside, and shrieked.

"What's wrong," asked Lucy from a ladder above. "Don't you like the color?" Pink stripes of paint, in streaky, unprofessional strokes, had been slapped over the bottom portion of the porch and Lucy was applying them above. "This is just the start. Your house really needs painting. And white's such an ordinary color. Pink's so much livelier." Below, Renaldo completed the desecration, smothering the house's former blankness.

"This is horrible," said Persephone. "Just horrible."

"Not as bad as your hair," said Lucy, as Persephone rushed inside.

"We'd better stop," said Renaldo.

"Why? I'll bet everyone else will like it." And she went on painting, dipping and stroking, dipping and stroking. Overhead the sun, which surprised with its brightness that morning, beat steadily, sucking the life from the last few drops of dew that clung to the morning grass. Above this grass paced Renaldo, holding his paintbrush in front of him like a sword to dispatch some imaginary foe.

Suddenly, Marmaduke burst through the front door. "What the Hell's going on," he demanded.

"We're just doing some painting," said Lucy.

"On our front porch? Without asking us? Without consulting the college? You have a lot of nerve!"

"It really did need painting," said Lucy forlornly. "And pink is a lovely color."

"Pink is a revolting color. And it should be up to us to decide, not you."

"Well," said Lucy, "I guess I should have asked first. But you needn't be so rude. I'm only trying to help."

"Help? You don't even know the meaning of the word. You come uninvited, stay God knows how long, mess the place up, leave dirty dishes in the sink, wake us up at night. And you expect us to understand? I'm going to have to ask you to leave."

"If that's how it has to be."

"That's how it has to be."

***

Renaldo rocked back and forth in the brown rocking chair in the living room, swaddling himself, like a lonely baby, like a fetus. Through the window, the sun's last rays filtered.

Through the door came Persephone. "Are you all right," she asked in a not unsympathetic voice, but perhaps not that sympathetic . "I found this on the porch, but it's covered in pink paint." She held out a now useless copy of *The Cat in the Hat Comes Back.*

"I'm fine," said Renaldo.

"Sorry we all had to be so rough on Lucy. But she really was impossible."

"That's how it goes, I guess."

And Persephone left Renaldo to the looming darkness, where he clutched the children's book ever more tightly, rocking forth and back, back and forth.

A Visit to Ramallah

. . . it seems to me a very old quarrel; I suppose it's in the blood, and perhaps will only end with it.

—Franz Kafka, "Jackals and Arabs"

January 11, 1984

"Alla Ramallah," Bernard told the portly taxi driver, thereby exhausting his entire vocabulary in Arabic. It worked; the taxi glided off, past the golden dome of the Temple of the Rock, through the narrow, winding streets, weaving between cars as aggressively as if driven by an Israeli; past turbaned Arabs pushing carts loaded with blankets and tapestries; past the black, shrouded forms of bearded Hasidic Jews; through thousands of years of history and strife; between and among the exhaust and honking of the motley vehicles that crowd Jerusalem's streets; through the eastern gates to that long and dusty and lonely road east. East, to the West Bank (or the occupied territories, or Judea and Samaria, depending on one's politics).

Alla Ramallah. To Ramallah. What simple yet magic words, rather like "Open Sesame," the gateway to a new world of possibilities. It was Bernard's second tiny linguistic triumph of the day. The first had happened as his friend, Judith, walked him to the bus from her small apartment. How strange these Israeli apartments are, Bernard had thought. They rose from the hills surrounding Jerusalem, vast hive-like complexes, functional yet strangely exotic, numbered in bizarre ways that only perplexed Bernard, as inscrutable as the magical numbering systems of the Jewish mystics. It was perplexingly easy to get lost among their dull towers and Judith had seemed annoyed at walking Bernard to the bus station, to "that **place** you're going," yet had refused to let him proceed alone. In the distance, along some stairwell, they had seen a gang of children, alive and bustling, engrossed in some activity. Bernard at first missed it, but Judith's sharp eyes had picked it up; they had captured a cat and were engaged in pulling it around by the tail, and Judith charged at them yelling: "Attem low chiot. Attem Yehudim."

Despite his minimal Hebrew, Bernard had actually picked up the meaning. "You are not animals. You are Jews." The intimidated children scattered and Judith hurried over to the animal. "Look at the poor creature!" she said. They had tied up its legs, but luckily Judith had a pocket knife with which she cut it free. They had even stuffed its mouth with cloth, which Judith pulled out in one swift motion. "Oh, how could they have done this?" She stroked the cat, which was fluffed with orange and yellow fur, while large, confused eyes stared at her. Its fur even seemed confused, out of joint, jagged and bedraggled. After a few seconds, it rose up and, with a half-hearted attempt at a "myeowr," bounded away.

"You can't believe these Israeli children," said Judith as they walked on. "They're just cruel. They torture animals. It must be the heat. They've all got sunstroke. They're crazy all the time."

As they reached the stop, the Israeli bus came blundering up the dusty road. "You're sure you want to go?" asked Judith as they ran for it. "Lord knows why."

Without replying, Bernard hopped on the bus. "Camah zeh Oleh," he asked the driver.

"One hundred shekels," the driver replied in English, with a laugh. The price had already leapt up twenty shekels. Who could keep up with Israel's mad currency?

The bus careened toward Jerusalem even more aggressively than usual, the driver a maniac among maniacs, sweeping past cars in the wrong lane as he swerved around curves, once nearly running head-on into a huge military truck. The radio blared throughout the bus, alternating the news (in Hebrew, of course) with Israeli and American pop. With astonishing speed, they entered Jerusalem. Bernard got off at the Arab quarter, into Jerusalem to leave Jerusalem, eastward to Palestine. From Jewish life to Arab. A crossing over.

He sunk back in the Arab cab, into a padded seat that must have been plush once, but now was nicked and bruised. The ride was astonishingly short, perhaps twenty minutes, into Ramallah, the putative heart (excepting Jerusalem) of a Palestinian state that had never actually existed, twenty minutes from one world into a total otherness. Yet an otherness that looked strangely the same, rows of white buildings growing like grim cacti in the desert, a functional, modern architecture alternating with older buildings. They pulled into the center of town; Bernard wordlessly paid a 100 shekel bill, received change, exited. He pulled out the instructions Annabelle had given to the Friends School, scrawled in pencil on a yellow sheet of paper. Not too difficult; just down the main avenue, a left turn, then a right one at a quirky angle.

The main avenue was strangely quiet. A squad of Israeli soldiers sauntered down the street, frumpled as usual though appearing more serious and alert than they would have within Israel proper, with rifles, like huge black wasp stings, slung over their soldiers. One block down, a couple of Arab women gazed shyly at Bernard's foreignness from their headdresses. Bernard took the two turns Annabelle had described and nearly bumped into a large sign featuring lovely Arabic script and, in smaller English letters, the words "Friends' School." It was a large brick building left over from the days of British colonialism. Almost before he rang the bell, Annabelle was at the door, greeting him with a hug. Annabelle's big hugs, he remembered from their college days, so unlike Judith, who always maintained a kind of icy distance from Bernard, while urging him to come to the college's Shabbat dinners. He went only once.

"Let me introduce you to everyone," Annabelle enthused. "This is my brother, Rob, and this is Hans." They all engaged in brief, limp handshakes. Annabelle was blonde and clean, her brother blonde and whiskered, Hans sloppy like an eternal student who spends too much time studying, no time grooming. Bernard surmised that they must all work for the Friends' School, probably as volunteers for a cause they believed in. After all, the Quakers had a longstanding relationship with the Palestinians, a fact that had bothered Judith when she was a student at their small Quaker college, but Bernard had barely noticed.

"There's food in the kitchen," said Annabelle. "Help yourself." The freshly baked bread complemented the olives and hummus and Bernard, famished, ate heartily, what could have been a prototypical Israeli meal. He was on the other side, yet somehow it was the same. Somehow, the kitchen reminded him of the college—makeshift but well furnished, with hearty pottery decorated in colorful patterns, with sturdy cutting boards and well-sharpened knives. The room, too, was large and sunny. The whole school, indeed, seemed rather luxurious, with tall ceilings and real wood floors, in contrast to the smaller, drabber buildings that Bernard had inhabited during his time in Israel. Bernard wondered briefly about the Palestinians—what were their homes like? Annabelle's companions seemed just scraggly enough to remind of his college days, but there was something stiff and distant about them.

Bernard entered the living room to a brief silence. Then the gang of them questioned him, in a slow, polite way, asking about his family, his hometown, how he'd liked college, what he'd majored in. Nothing about his stay in Israel. They kept up the small talk for about half an hour, then Rob and Hans retreated to a large room down the hall. Bernard and Annabelle reminisced about college for a time, then swapped gossip about their old friends. Bernard was surprised by how much Annabelle knew; he, himself, barely kept up. What little he was able to inform her of concerned friends who had gone to large graduate schools in the Midwest. She, on the other hand, knew of one old friend who'd gone to Nicaragua to work with the Sandinistas, another in California helping the farmworkers, a third who'd joined the Peace Corps (a politically questionable organization in her estimation). When they'd run out of gossip, there was a brief silence, then suddenly Annabelle leapt up excitedly. "Wait, I've got a surprise for you." And she popped in a tape, one of their old favorites, UB40 singing "Tyler is guilty, white judge has said so." Bernard didn't have the heart to tell her it was one of four tapes he'd brought to Israel and he was so sick of it he'd be more than happy to smash it to small pieces with a hammer.

Annabelle had some evening work, editing articles for the Palestinian newspaper *Al Fajir,* so Bernard said he'd like to read, then go to bed. Annabelle provided him with a long swath of mosquito netting. "You'll need this for sure," she said. "The mosquitos are atrocious." Then she disappeared into her room. As Bernard passed the living room on the way to the bathroom, he heard Rob and Hans talking and laughing while soft music played. Wisps of smoke carried the pungent aroma of marijuana into the hall.

At first, Bernard didn't bother to cover himself with the netting, since it seemed uncomfortable and mosquitos rarely bothered him. On this night, though, he soon felt a few little bites, but, since he was already half asleep, he didn't want to bother pulling up the protective screen. His thoughts turned to Annabelle. Her family, she had told him once, had actually been in Palestine in 1948 when the British left and war arrived—her father was some kind of scholar. Bernard reflected on how, on a trip to a nearby lake, amid friends, she had mentioned, buoyantly, her father reading her the book *Good Night Moon,* a thoughtful moment when she wasn't making sharp-edged comments about politics. She had been a normal kid with normal feelings, love for her father.

He drifted into sleep, only to awake to itching and irritation—he could feel the little bastards crawling on his skin. He brushed some away, too tired and slow to smash them. Finally, he turned on the light and undertook the cumbersome process of pulling all the material around him, although it was hard to avoid cracks. As he attempted to sleep, he felt the bites accumulating.

And so it continued throughout the night, in and out of sleep, incessant biting and itching. Only once did he manage to squash one of the creatures, which was engorged with blood. His own blood, he realized. It was almost as if he were squashing himself.

From the kitchen, voices drifted, but now the mosquitos had quieted, and it seemed his only chance to sleep. The morning light wasn't enough to dissuade. The voices continued, got louder, would lull briefly then, as he'd start to sleep, one would rise excitedly and angrily. Or laugh violently at some joke. Most often, he recognized the offending voice as Hans's. Finally, he gave up on sleep, rose and dressed groggily, and stumbled into the kitchen. The room quieted. Bernard told them to keep speaking, not to let him bother them.

"We've been discussing the situation of the Palestinians," said Hans. "And, since you're obviously a supporter of Israel, we don't want to argue with you. It would be three against one."

Bernard thought of protesting, of telling them to keep talking. Instead, he said, "Well, I'm not absolutely in favor of Israel. They've done a lot wrong. You really can't split the situation so easily into one side or the other. It's not that simple."

"In this case," said Hans, "it is that simple. Israel is the occupier, the Palestinians the victims who were driven out of their homes."

"We'd better make plans for the day," Annabelle leapt in. "I have to work in the afternoon"—she peered earnestly at Bernard—"but I can spend time with you till then." They decided to play badminton. Luckily, there was a net outdoors.

Bernard couldn't believe how serious the game was. In college, he and Annabelle had played a few times, mainly hitting back and forth, not caring who won. Now, however, they engaged in a bitter duel. And yes, the mosquito bites stung as sweat dripped over them. Yes, the heat was bitter, dry, cruel, and unyielding. Annabelle was a much steadier player, so Bernard tried to offset this with a combination of overhead blasts and odd, spinning shots. On his overheads, however, the birdie tended to catch in the mesh of his racket, which was old. This threw off his rhythm, but worse, he was out of practice, and Annabelle won the first game. He fought ferociously to win the second, but was so tired and overheated that she easily beat him in the third.

"Let's go inside," she said, cheerfully. "Better not to overdo it." He felt dizzy and, back in the kitchen, she handed him a huge glass of lemonade. "Better watch it. You might get sunstroke. Happens a lot around here. With this dryness, you aren't aware of how overheated you are. The sun can drive people crazy."

She had to leave to teach a class, and Bernard settled in for an afternoon with the books and newspapers scattered around the house, most of which found a different twist on attacking the Zionist, imperialist, militarist, racist, expansionist, Jewish Israeli state.

Bernard felt a slight nausea and dizziness; he knew it was from the heat, but didn't feel like sleeping or drinking fluids. Unable to concentrate on the unpleasant reading material, he pondered the mystery of Annabelle. In college, she had always been running off to protests even though, with the Vietnam War long over and the Civil Rights Act safely passed, the era of protest seemed over. They were part of a generation that slipped through the cracks of history. But there was always injustice—workers being underpaid and mistreated, conflict somewhere in the world that the U.S. had something to do with. Bernard finally went along to a little protest when Jimmy Carter reinstated the need to register for the draft.

It was still a bit of a mystery to Bernard how he had ended up in a house of activists, at the fringe of their circle, his senior year. He enjoyed history, mostly the Greeks and Romans, as a kind of mythology. Only at the end of college did he start to find connections to real human events. Honor is always usurped by tribalism and the thirst for blood. Was that history's great lesson?

That evening he made plans to travel with Annabelle and Rob to Jerusalem the next day. Soon it would all be over; he would escape from Palestine unscathed. That night, he had his last dinner there, the first in which they all ate together; he and Annabelle; blonde, cherubic Rob; and slovenly Hans whose eyes seemed always tired, who spoke in a ponderous voice as though every topic touched him to the gut. When Bernard complained about the mosquitos, Rob explained that they had special electrical gadgets to keep the creatures away, although unfortunately there wasn't one for Bernard. The conversation floundered along, Anabelle, Rob and Hans discussing their daily activities which, since they were all concerned with the Palestinians, skirted political controversy without quite touching it. Finally, Bernard, feeling the night trickling away while he barely spoke, brought up his job on the Kibbutz picking olives.

"You realize," said Hans in a demanding voice, "that by working on a Kibbutz you're supporting an economy that exploits Palestinians."

"I thought we'd agreed not to discuss this," said Annabelle.

"No, I want to know. Bernard's in Palestine, but he hasn't explained what he's doing here. It's relevant."

"Anyway," said Annabelle, "just by paying taxes in America, or just about anywhere, you're supporting the military and lots of other terrible things. It can't be avoided."

"Israel is a special case. Aside from the Palestinians, look at Israel's relationship with South Africa. Look at their bombing of Lebanon. How can you excuse a nation that does this?"

"Israel's lived under the gun a long time," said Bernard, feeling a quiver in his voice. "They've been pushed. So now you have a government that feels it needs to be aggressive. A mistaken government, maybe, but just a temporary aberration. The Labor Party will win again."

"The Labor Party's no different. It is the same group that founded Israel."

"All of Israel's previous wars have been in self-defense."

"That's a Zionist myth. Israel attacked first in every war up to 1973."

Bernard didn't know what to say. This contradicted everything he'd always heard, but now he wasn't sure what was a lie and what the truth. He wished he knew more history. "What about 1948?" he said limply.

"The Jews struck first. And in '56 they joined in the British imperialist war for the Suez Canal, which even the U.S. opposed."

"That's not what I've always heard. Anyway, things will be different when the Labor Party returns to power."

"And how do you know your precious Labor Party will win the next election?"

"It has to happen. It's the only sane thing and Israel is a sane country."

"Not true. Israel is a psychopathological country. I have a book that proves this. It's a country obsessed with the Holocaust, believing itself cursed with eternal suffering. So it transfers its hatred onto the Palestinians, who had nothing to do with the Holocaust. They are the real victims. Israel is sick at the root and has been since its creation."

"At its creation the Arabs invaded it from three directions."

"As I said, the Jews struck first."

"Enough!" shouted Annabelle with surprising venom. "We're not going to solve any of this now. Let's all just be rational."

"Are the Israelis rational," said Hans, "when they break the bones of a Palestinian child?"

"Let's just all shut up."

The mosquitos were brutal that night. After some futile scratching and swatting, and repeated attempts to draw the net tighter around him, Bernard fell into dreamless slumber. His sleep was so deep and so black that, in the morning, he couldn't believe he awoke. Annabelle's voice drew him softly from the darkness. "Wake up. We're going to Jerusalem."

As Bernard ate breakfast, Annabelle apologized for Hans' behavior. Then, just as they were leaving, Hans came in, absent the cocky demeanor Bernard had, in just a couple of days, learned to expect. "Listen," he said. "I'm sorry if I got out of hand last night. It's just that I'm so concerned over the plight of the Palestinians." And he shook Bernard's hand firmly. Bernard, however, just stood limply, letting Hans pump his arm vigorously. He felt as though his fingers were being crushed. Then Hans retreated to his room.

As Bernard, Annabelle, and Rob prepared to leave, Hans came running out for a quick goodbye, offering a hug which Annabelle returned in a reluctant fashion.

In a blink, the taxi took them into Jerusalem's ancient walls. They walked through the narrow, crowded streets of the Arab quarter. Annabelle spoke in her limited Arabic, friendly and smiling, to the Arab vendors in the street. They switched immediately to English, and Annabelle bargained for a bright red scarf, finally paying a rather high price. "I'm so glad I'm with a man," she said. "In this culture, it's difficult to be a woman alone—they so easily misunderstand you. All they know about American women is from the movies."

They detoured into the Christian quarter, to the Church of the Holy Sepulchre. Inside, two wizened nuns peered kindly from stark garments, looking as though they'd stood there as long as the church. Which might as well have been forever. Bernard wondered at the building's huge, arching structure, which seemed somehow more spiritual, although darker and less grand, than other churches and mosques he'd been in.

Afterward, they skipped the Jewish quarter entirely, heading back to the Arab quarter, where they ate a quintessential Israeli meal of falafel and humus, replete with olives, which Bernard gulped down hungrily. Next was the Dome of the Rock, but they were turned back at the gate since it was closed. "That's unusual," said Annabelle. "It's past the noontime prayer." Bernard didn't tell her, but he'd been there before and it had been closed then, too; to him, the Golden Dome remained unbreachable.

Finally, almost as though by accident, they approached the Wailing Wall. To Bernard it was just a wall, old and cracked and rather ordinary. This was a rather ordinary day, and the crowd was sparse—a few tourists, snapping pictures—the lines nonexistent, with just a couple of people bowed in prayer at each part of the wall, the men's and the women's. As they gazed down at thousands of years of history, Anabelle spoke. "I've heard that Jews get very emotional at the Wailing Wall. Some even cry. Does it do anything to you?"

"Nothing," said Bernard. "But then my family's not religious. We're lost Jews. I'm not even sure why I came to Israel."

They stared just a few minutes more. "Why are the men separate from the women?" asked Rob.

"That's part of the Jewish religion. Men and women are separate at a holy place. It's that way in orthodox synagogues, too."

"What a sexist religion." It's that way in Islam, too, Bernard thought, but did not say.

They bought some bread rolls from an Arab vendor and, sitting on the steps, munched them lethargically as a group of Israeli soldiers passed in front of them. Finally, Rob spoke again.

"Well, I guess I'll go see the wall." He rose up and Annabelle and Bernard followed. The line had lengthened and they stood waiting to get to the wall itself. "Are you going too?" he asked Bernard.

"No. I've already been."

Rob spotted a vendor selling cardboard hats. "What are those for?" he asked.

"You need them to go to the wall if you don't already have a yarmulka."

"Well, forget that." And Rob marched defiantly away. Disheartened, Annabelle stepped out of the line also.

They lingered in Jerusalem a while longer, sauntering aimlessly through the old city. No one was sure who was leading and who following, and indeed several times they set out in different directions. Bernard would turn and follow his companions, but even Annabelle and Rob seemed out of sync, neither sure where the other was going or who should follow. Finally, Annabelle announced that she had to get back to Ramallah and they headed toward a cab stand. She gave Bernard one of her big hugs, and even a timid kiss on the cheek. Then she and Rob disappeared into the cab.

Bernard felt somehow empty, like he'd lost something, but he didn't know what. Mosquito bites lined his chest, climbed his shoulder, and culminated in a batter of bites under his left armpit. He became increasingly aware of the bites and began to scratch compulsively as blood oozed out. He walked and itched and scratched and itched. Finally, he just stood there in some dark corner of the Arab quarter, scratching and scratching incessantly, until he'd popped the biggest bite, right under his armpit, and salty sweat seeped in, and he felt a mixture of sweat and hair and blood. He took out his hand and peered at the streaks of blood upon his fingers. Then he began to suck, and the sweat and blood tasted salty and good. But he worried that he'd give himself some strange disease. Some bacteria lingering from Ramallah's alien air. So he walked on through twisting streets beneath the darkening Jerusalem sky. Finally, as he was returning to the city's center to catch the bus, a young man in a faded shirt popped out of the shadows.

"It is not people Jewish," he said, peering at Bernard with forlorn eyes. "It is people Palestinian." Not replying, Bernard walked briskly on.

The bus took him swiftly to the apartment complex at the edge of Jerusalem. He rang the doorbell, but no one seemed home. He rang again, then, just as he turned around, it swung open. Judith stood before him with big, tired eyes, her red hair curling and disheveled.

"So," she said sternly. "You made it back. I hope you had a good time with Annabelle and her friends. I guess they're your friends now."

"Not really."

"There's a little dinner left, though it's cold."

Bernard ate in silence while Judith read in the next room. Then he washed up his few dishes. Something about Judith's room seemed ominous and unapproachable, so he just sat there on the living-room couch. Finally, Judith came out, bearing sheets. "I'm tired," she said. "I have a lot to do tomorrow. I'm going to bed."

"All right."

"So, how did they treat you on the West Bank?" she asked in a disinterested voice.

"All right. Well, Anabelle was nice, but not the others. I don't know. I guess they sort of tried to be friendly."

"I'm not surprised. You know what you were? You were a token Jew."

"I don't think that's really right."

"I don't see why you had to go to the West Bank in the first place."

"It's a good idea to get to the Palestinian side."

"They don't have a side. They never suffered the Holocaust. They don't have 3000-year roots on the land."

"I guess."

"You know what Annabelle and her crowd reminded me of in college? They were like children."

"How so?"

"Playing at some game they don't understand. What do they know about the Middle East? What stake do they have in it?"

"They did come all the way to the West Bank."

"And when they're done they'll go back to their nice comfortable lives. What do they know about the Jews? What right have they to judge us? Did they even try the least iota to understand us?"

"I guess not."

"Of course not. Well, I've got to get to bed. I'll see you in the morning."

And she left Bernard on the couch. He was alone, but the sheets were clean and there was a pleasant, cool breeze and, best of all, no mosquitos. Still, itching with a burning sensation that seemed to penetrate deep within him, seemed as if it would last forever, he tumbled into an ambivalent sleep.

Julie in Hell

Hell surrounds me and I am creating it, out of freshly painted oils, out of ceramics. The smell of linseed oil hangs and mingles with dust particles, has become the tainted air I breath. Demons with pitchforks stab naked men and women as they have since time immemorial, or at least since the start of the Christian era. And my hands are shaping it. Does this make me God? Does it make me Satan?

This stately little starter house was only meant to be temporary. At least that was Oliver's plan. I had thought it equipped with everything to be our little paradise on Earth—although now it's my own little hell. Oliver always wanted to move on to a larger house, a massive mansion, not this stunted facsimile. He's moved on, all right, just in time to escape the pandemic.

What did I do to him but love him too much? Or at least stand by him? Or at least lust for him? Or at least put up with his affairs, which he started from day one? Or at least I've decided that he had all these affairs, but that's speculation, perhaps vengeful speculation. He did disappear at strange hours, sometimes for days, but it could, I suppose, have been for work, as he claimed.

Oliver always wanted more. More money, a home fitness center, the latest marvel from Apple every year, hundred-year-old Scotch, a Mercedes, a Tesla. Perhaps that was part of his charm. I should have been warned—or taken the warning seriously—shortly after we started dating and he was rhapsodizing that if he could make a billion dollars, he would die a happy man. I made that classic mistake every woman makes, thinking I could change him, temper his greed, enhance his green-eyed roguishness. Besides, that little lick of blond in his hair conveyed a certain flair, an unconventional spirit.

One day, shortly after our marriage, I walked in on him straining and gasping in our new home gym, flat on his back pushing up weights in those little red shorts that drove me crazy, shining with sweat. "Yo, Julie," he said, not angry, "you caught me by surprise." He had never wanted me to see him sweat, enjoyed seeming confident and effortless, beautiful. But somehow he didn't mind now. I took it as a sign that he had relaxed, shown off his vulnerable side, that we were truly married.

They were so different from art school, those men at Wharton. So confident, so groomed, such a bunch of frat boys. So cocky and masculine. Everything I'd hated or had pretended to hate but found strangely compelling. My split personality. So different from the few disorganized, aimless boys I'd dated before. Such as Ralph, who wanted to marry me.

At art school, I was always different. The one who tidied up, did dishes, even swept the floor once in a while at our overstuffed McMansion, already dilapidated, packed with slovenly students, each with our own dream. We all go in expecting to be the next Frida Kahlo and come out struggling for a living wage. I knew by the end of my first semester that I was a failure as an artist, but still survived three years immersed in paint and clay doing just enough to pass. Then straight to another city, an elite MBA program, two years of ambivalence and hard work, followed by a degree.

It was shitty to leave Ralph with a single text, refusing to answer his frantic calls and messages, day after day, week after week. But I never promised him anything, never even agreed that we were an official couple. And he was so needy, always asking what I thought of his art. I could call it clever, I could call it strange, original, thought-provoking. He'd look at me with those gaping eyes, holes into an empty soul, always pleading for vindication, asking for more. I had nothing to give.

Strange, perhaps cosmically just, but rather mundane, that Oliver left me in exactly the same way I left Ralph. Even though deep inside

I'd started to question the marriage, when the fatal text arrived I wept for days, barely ate or slept. Did Oliver find me needy and mundane, like I had found Ralph? But I didn't ask for much, worked and cooked and cleaned for Oliver, enough to faintly begin to resent him. Most likely, Oliver ultimately found me ordinary, not quite posh enough, brash enough, lovely enough, glamorous enough, with my brown hair and big butt. The weight charts put me just barely at healthy, but I never quite trust them.

And now I'm alone in the midst of a pandemic with nothing but an MFA, an MBA, and a job that pays nicely and that I can do safely from my home computer. Which is a lot, I know, compared to so many.

An MFA. An MBA. Two sides of a split personality. An MFAMBA. An emfambya, as I affectionately call it, my twin achievements in this still youngish life.

My marriage at least made it a year. One year, one month, one week, and one day. And perhaps one hour. That's a bit of an achievement, I guess.

Perhaps what's most wounded is my pride. Oliver just used me as a stepping stone. My safe job meant he could take risks, start his own company speculating on currency and God knows what else, with me as a fallback while he won and lost money at the financial casino. But he won more than he lost. Won enough to finally leave me.

My day job is so rational, so organized. Marketing takes just a bit of organization, a bit of imagination, and returns a nice life. Best of all, you can do it from home—at least during the pandemic.

But I'm so lonely. I feel like the loneliest person in this time of great loneliness. Perhaps I should have married Ralph. He, at least, would have stayed with me. That's more important than love. Or lust, which might have been all I ever had.

Ralph, with the pot belly hanging off his scrawny frame, with the prematurely thinning hair and tacky pop t-shirts, with his strange videos that combined spasmodic animation and real life. Scenes of death—flowers fading, brown grasslands, frogs being dissected, road kill—set to schmaltzy love music. Ralph was certain he was a genius. Perhaps he was right, but sometimes I wondered how he got into art school in the first place.

In the pandemic, art has saved me. I suppose it's rather trite art—all these demons poking and prodding at naked souls licked by flames, eaten by worms and snakes. Hieronymus Bosch did it so much better. But hey, I'm doing it multi-media, transforming my entire house with a maze of paintings and statues. Isn't that imaginative? Isn't that original? Professor Fortunati would give me at least a B+. Like she did on my MFA thesis.

My house was meant to be a little heaven—high, creamy ceilings, golden trim, velvety red curtains, a grand picture window. I fought with Oliver over every puny detail, and most of the time he won. But hey, at least he smiled as he got his way, never got angry, the art of the soft sell. He was a great salesman, mostly of himself. Always so patient and empathetic, at least externally—was he just hiding an inner compulsion to dominate? And I loved the house despite its excesses, although I doubt Fortunati would have given it even a B+. Trite, she would have called it. There are so many ways of being trite.

Still, this triteness was my own little heaven. The basic structure is still intact, although I've removed bricks from the fireplace, dug out plaster bit by painful bit and even sawed through drywall when necessary, desiccated parts of the house to make way for various statues and reliefs, some still just contemplated. I got a little overzealous in my destruction.

Through a hole in the wall a beam of light shines, a hole awaiting my next little masterpiece, a snaky creature, feminine with huge breasts visible inside the house and an enormous bum that sticks out to the world. The fireplace is only partly reconstructed as an altar, a place of worship. Bricks remain scattered about, perhaps to build something new. Art eats away from within, like maggots in the gut.

There's an idea for a Ralph piece. Come to think of it, didn't he do a short piece on maggots, with "What a Wonderful World" playing in the background? Just after Oliver left, I called and texted Ralph repeatedly. Divine retribution? No answer. Please, please, I'm desperate, I scrawled in one text, desiring Ralph's clumsy, needy comfort for at least one night. But after my initial week of panic, I gave up. Why would he want me? And do I want him?

My messages to Oliver, on the other hand, continued for at least a month, slowly fading away with my hope, fading like the health and happiness of a nation stricken by plague.

Do I love myself? Do I hate myself? Somehow, I still love my transitory house, that part that appears solid and real, seems to protect me.

I don't love Oliver anymore, or at least the anger is greater than the love. I hope Margret is happy, at least for now. I never met her, the woman who replaced me. Margret. A posher, sexier name than mine, doubtless a posher, sexier woman. He'll end up leaving her, too. Trite. At least I got the house. But my failure eats away at me.

Oliver was trite, too. More money, more women, undoubtedly grabbing pussy just like Trump wherever you can get it, a frat boy's dream. But he did bring me to ecstasy, unlike those boys I'd previously dated. He always did have that patient and pleasing side, touching me in all the right places just like I asked and more. I'm sure he's proud of that, getting women to moan in ecstasy. I'm sure he's spent years counting the numbers, just like he counts his finances. If there were a prize for women moaning, he'd mount it in his new house with his new woman, both much finer than me, I am certain. Till he moves on to a still bigger house, a still blonder woman with bigger boobs, a smaller waist.

I did love the house. And I still love the yard with its bunnies and robins and sparrows and chipmunks. Even the squirrels are good friends, the only friends I have. Perhaps it's a bit generic, a bit of an every-yard—Oliver cared about the yard less than the house itself, never added his ornate touches. So it's mine, and it's filled with life. And the house is mine, too.

While out planting the garden one fine evening, near the start of the pandemic, I collapsed in tears into the dirt, watering the nascent veggies with salt and loneliness. When I looked up, a rabbit spoke to me. "Julie," she said, "only art can save your life." Next morning, bright at 6 AM, I got on Amazon and ordered paint, turpentine, linseed oil (no flat, ugly acrylics for me—I want something that shines with passion), clay, even a little kiln of my own. And so my artistic rampage began. The kiln still shines brightly in what's left of the fireplace.

So why am I destroying it, at least on the inside? Bit by bit, painting by painting, clay statue by clay statue. In the front room, a shiny blue demon stretches a woman on a rack, her joints popping out. In a busted-out portion of wall, horned snakes slither, bulging with the humans they've consumed—in the center, a woman's legs kick in agony, her head and torso already swallowed by a massive serpent. And on and on, in every room. My energy consumed, night after night, in artistic agony of creation.

There are so many ways to make devils, so many skin tones, so many ways to proportion their heads, to extend their ears, to add horns unobtrusive or ornate. Not that many ways to depict people being tortured, although perhaps I just lack the imagination.

And why should people suffer so? Why is our whole species fascinated with horror movies, S & M, torture camps? What's wrong with me? What's wrong with us?

I bought blackout curtains for the picture window. My satanic art is best enjoyed in the gloom.

Now, naked and spattered with red paint, I stand before my grandest creation that dominates the fireplace at the center of the Great Room, the kiln flickering in the background—Satan himself, bloated, wearing two proud, erect cow horns, his face a cross between a fat goat and Oliver's rugged visage, horns scraping the ceiling, staring up at the heaven he can never attain. I prostrate myself at His feet, kiss His cloven hooves.

Soon, I think, I will destroy him.

Metafictional Interlude

I'm My Own Author

I am the author of my own story. I don't know how it happened and I don't want it to be this way. I am in the midst of a passionate love affair that will end badly, though I haven't yet decided how. I must write more backstory so that I can understand not only myself, but my lover, Juliet. Yes, I picked the most obvious name, however I'm not calling myself Romeo, but Morton. Morton and Juliet, almost a comic effect. How can this be a grand and tragic love story? Yet it will be that, but also, I hope, tremendously funny as my hopes and dreams are crushed. By a series of external events? By my own character flaws? By Juliet being so, so different from what she first appeared? I'm still in the process of working this out.

I'm doing all this to please my audience. And who are they? I don't know, at least not yet. As the author of my own story, do I have the agency to bring the audience into being? Or are they pre-existing, my reason for writing? I won't know that for a long, long time, long after Juliet and I have been hopelessly ripped apart. This must be an ongoing story, a novel or perhaps a trilogy. It will be epic. As the author, I have decided that. Or perhaps that will unfold as I write. Or it has been decided for me by some outside force, perhaps a publisher. Have I already signed a contract? That is undecided as I have not yet written backstory. Or is the publisher something outside the story itself? But how can the story exist without a publisher to bring it to an audience? An existential crisis! I'm obviously early in the writing process. I hope, believe, and pray that all will be revealed as the novel—or trilogy, quartet, or whatever—unfolds. Of course, I am deciding it all, which means that I will eventually decide how and why I was born and grew up. My origin. My back story.

What about Juliet, my one great love (at least in this first part of the ongoing story)? How will I develop her? What are the intricacies of her character? Or even her major features, her motivation? Why am I—or will I be—so consumed by her? I can make her Polish. Zalinski. That means she's most likely Catholic. And since I'm Morton, I'm Jewish. Morton Lipschutz. That means religion will come between us. But perhaps just in a light, comic way as I might decide that neither of us is particularly religious. Maybe I'll make myself an atheist and Juliet a lapsed Catholic with a spiritual worldview. She might even believe in astrology, mediums and such, while I am a skeptic. This could be a source of friction between us.

My this is fun! The ability to invent details, whatever I want, to play god. Though I'm deliberately giving "god" a small "g" as I'm far from important enough to call myself God. Of course, I want the story, or novel, or series, or whatever it is, to be good, ideally great (at least I'll aim for greatness, probably achieve mediocrity), which means that everything has to be at the service of plot and character development, to grip the reader and keep her turning pages—even if electronic ones. There's that reader again, getting in the way. What's the point of having godlike powers if you're always using them to please some theoretical audience? Why do I go to so much trouble to placate these people I don't even know (or other intelligent beings, if I want to go the sci-fi route)?

Anyway, back to Juliet. If she believes in mystical mumbo jumbo, perhaps she is also a naturalist, a vegan, a yogi, and an anti-Vaxxer. This could be what drives us apart, particularly as the story proceeds? Perhaps she refuses to get the Covid vaccine, while I am first in line, maybe even jumping the gun, finding a way to get the shot before others who need it more. Maybe I'm a bit of a sneak and a manipulator. It's a better story if we're both flawed, but in radically different ways. Maybe Juliet is a highly ethical person, but naïve, a bit of a klutz, while I'm a hard-edged, radical skeptic who doesn't have the sympathy for her that I should. But she is endangering me, and other people, by refusing to get vaccinated.

My, I've gotten the two of us into a conundrum—good for keeping the reader hooked—but there's one huge narrative problem. What drew us together in the first place? Was it just her wholesome looks, her healthy red cheeks and hair, her innocent naivete? Maybe she mistook me for a sympathetic fellow because I played along with her spiritualism, pretended to think that the stars do, indeed, guide our destinies, as I chatted with her at some party, revealed tidbits from my past (which I still have to invent) just to get her into bed. That makes sense, as I'm a bit of a scoundrel. But now I've worked myself into a frenzy, thinking of her lovely flesh and flashing green eyes (perhaps she'll have to be Irish and not Polish) and I really am hot for her. The imagination is a powerful thing—it has me all excited over this disembodied figment. I'd better do more to give her flesh and character and appeal. The initial scene where we meet has to be just right to get the audience believing, sympathetic to both characters, rooting for us. But the inevitable end has to be worked into the beginning—though the audience won't know it until the tragic breakup actually occurs after I, the author, have worked them into a sympathetic frenzy. Unfortunately, as my own author, I'll be suffering through all these twists and turns.

And how did I come to be my own author in the first place? I don't know that yet, won't know until multitudes of words come spewing out of my fingertips onto the electronic pages, won't know until after multiple revisions. Heck, I don't even know if this is going to be published serially, or if I have to work the entire manuscript out first. I prefer serial, as otherwise it's simply too overwhelming. But what does my publisher want? And who is the publisher and am I authoring this publisher into being? But then why did I begin writing this in the first place? Had I already created the publisher or did the publisher solicit me?

I don't know, I don't know, I don't know, and it's killing me. I feel like smacking my head against a wall. Will I answer profound questions about the nature of being? Or am I going down a rabbit-hole obsessing over the audience and publisher? Shouldn't I just tell a good story?

Perhaps my atheism will come out in an ugly statement during a fight over something stupid? Say, whether a coffee cup that Juliet dropped so that it shattered across the kitchen floor, fragments swimming among hot java, was preordained, filled with meaning, or just an act of physics. She'll see it as a sign, I'll call her a stupid klutz and explain it as the laws of physics. I'll leave it to her to clean up, weeping, as I'm a bit of a sexist—but then again, she's the one who broke it, isn't she? I'll have an important research project to finish upstairs, but really I'll be sneaking e-mails to my other lover, Roxanne, while Juliet sweeps away the last few fragments then cries herself to sleep on the couch. Or perhaps she'll walk in on me in the middle of one of these letters. But I'm crafty and have recently rearranged the room so that the computer screen faces away from the door, giving me time to switch screens. Still, she's grown suspicious and will eventually sneak onto the computer and find her way onto my secret e-mail account filled with love letters, plus evidence of a financial scam I'm involved in. Did she wangle the password from me, or was I careless and left the window with the secret e-mails open? Perhaps I secretly wanted to be discovered? Was it through guilt or to end a relationship I was secretly sick of, a secret even to myself?

My, what an cad I am, willing to sneak off with a lover in the midst of a pandemic and risk infecting myself and Juliet. Romeo would be ashamed! But, as an author, I'll be sowing the seeds of a failed relationship, portraying great transgressions alongside petty domestic fights, showing the many ways a love affair deteriorates and finally shatters.

In any case, the shattered coffee cup does have meaning beyond the laws of physics, though not in the way Juliet thinks. It symbolizes the state of our relationship. It symbolizes my corrupt soul. I think this symbol even arose organically from the story, rather than being imposed, a sign of a truly great author! Or at least a pretty good one? Or perhaps it is a rather trite symbol, after all?

And is the research project that I was working on upstairs really a financial scam? Or is it actually this book? Am I sacrificing for my art, sacrificing my great love, my own soul, for a chance at immortality as an author? Is the character in the book writing me? Or is he too busy being a scoundrel? Am I a separate consciousness writing a myself who's not really me? But doesn't he have to, in a way, be me? Can I write myself into being or did my consciousness preexist? Perhaps it needed to exist for eternity. I certainly can't remember a beginning, but then how could I if I didn't exist prior to the beginning?

I'd better keep writing so that, eventually, I find out. I'm really excited about the first task—getting myself and Juliet into bed! Perhaps I'm my only audience, so I'd better be excited enough to begin that first scene. I'm going to need to keep at it so that I can reach the point, in the distant, distant future, where all is explained. It all begins with Juliet, but it will end with something very distant that I can only barely begin to perceive.

Eternity

It was a day with no beginning, no ending, only middle. Interminable hours in the lab, an incessant evening crunching data. At 2 AM, Marissa tumbled into insomnia, her brain still juiced. Her beagle, Lucy, snuggled beside her with a delicate whimpering. Stroking Lucy's flank and belly, Marissa repeated her secret word to calm her hyperactive mind. Briefly, she sensed sleep coming, but a violent sneeze from Lucy re-awoke her.

More violent than a lightening flash, an idea disturbed the bleak, black night. A vaccine against death. For nearly two decades, Marissa had been researching the ravages of aging, possible cures for diseases that hobble the mind and send one into an ugly, angry version of second childhood. But, she suddenly realized, she hadn't been audacious enough. Science had advanced to the point where death itself could be conquered.

Details of how such a vaccine could be produced came to her as if in a waking dream, a universal vaccine to heighten the sensitivity of red corpuscles, white blood cells, the heart, kidney, liver, the very brain itself, the delicate, sinuous nervous system. Humans had unlocked the code of life, could play with it, alter it, halt the machinery of degeneration.

Yes, it must be theoretically possible, using the latest genetics, the clean, obscene power of CRISPR technology. A simple shot or two, perhaps an occasional booster, would end humanity's greatest terror.

Brilliant! She would be immortal in the annals of science. But wait— she would be immortal in actuality, too, once she was inoculated by her own vaccine. Inoculated from death? What an awe-inspiring phrase.

Thoughts seethed through the long night. What would it be like to be immortal? With a shock, she realized, she was now in a position to find out. She, herself, would not die. A whole planet of people never aging, never decaying.

Of course, that would make the issue of childbirth . . . problematic? If the planet's population were to go ever up, what would that mean for the future? How would the world's bounteous, but not unlimited, resources provide for our ever-growing species? Marissa had, in recent years, been worrying ever more about climate change, species extinction, chemicals permeating our air and water. We are a rapacious species. Did we deserve this gift that no other creature possessed, immortality?

There was one being, simple and wonderful, who did deserve eternal life. Her sweet, lovely Lucy, who even now nuzzled her. When her last dog had died, Marissa was so grief-stricken she almost didn't get another, but oh how lonely her nights would be without Lucy. Had she so given herself to her life as a scientist, she wondered, as to sacrifice marriage. Perhaps Lucy could be her companion forever.

Of course, that wouldn't happen. Nobody would endorse precious vaccines for dogs and cats when there were billions of humans waiting desperately for eternal life. Except, perhaps, for the beloved dogs and cats of billionaires. When you have enough money, an exception can always be found. People are such an unfair species, so selfish.

Eternal life. What would one think of over the centuries? The millennia? Would one simply turn over the same thoughts again and again? An earworm, "Whoops, I Did It Again," that she knew was a bit tacky, had been plaguing Marissa for the last several weeks. What would it mean to think of that song for, say, a billion years? Whoops, I did it again and again and again, forever and ever.

Eternity couldn't mean eternity, could it? Surely something would come along, a meteor, perhaps, and end it all? And our own species was capable of destroying itself. Hadn't we invented nuclear bombs? A wonder we hadn't already blown ourselves up, along with much of the life on this planet, including many innocent and wonderful species that deserved to live far more than humanity. And would we really grow wiser as we aged? Marissa had noticed that, instead of learning, people would harden their positions, grow, in a way, more cynical, repeat the same mistakes over and over. Or, without neural degeneration, would people develop a tempered wisdom, a deeper knowledge of self and ability to guide the young, as the elderly are supposed to? Biology was mysterious, absurdly complex, yet solvable. People were a problem without a solution.

Had Marissa been snoozing when light crept through the blinds? Did she really want to survive another endless day? Perhaps she would call in sick? She was killing herself, killing herself. Her work had seemed so vital, worth the male colleagues who leapfrogged her. Her old lab partner, Ralph Bunchstein, even "borrowed" her idea for a theoretical pathway to reducing Alzheimers, got important publications out of it. The fat, pathetic toad. Perhaps she should sympathize with him, that he talked with a lisp, walked with a limp, but she despised him. He was now at Harvard, while she was stuck as an Associate Professor at a not quite first-tier school (but still a Research One institution). She was smarter, worked harder, than her colleagues, but where was her reward? People did not deserve immortal life. Marissa would get her revenge, leave our species to grow old, face our end, as we deserved. She would not reveal the road map to a vaccine for death. Its secret would die with her.

Whoops, I Did It Again—would that song never stop plaguing her? Was this what geniuses thought? Whoops, I Did It Again, I created eternal life. Britney Spears, another woman whose talent was stolen and exploited by a man.

Unusually, Lucy had crept away in the night. Did she no longer love Marissa? Was the poor dog ill? Shocked at her aloneness, Marissa sat bolt upright to face a new day.

Marissa would get her revenge. Now was her chance at greatness, proof she was the most brilliant of the brilliant. She would work harder than ever, work herself to death, to eternal life, just to prove she was more ingenious than her male colleagues, exponentially more so than Bunchstein. He would be forgotten. Marissa's name would shimmer in the celestial sphere of the gods alongside Einstein and Newton. Damn the consequences.

She arose to her first day as a God, her first day of eternity.

The Literalist

The Literalist was trapped. Trapped for all eternity. The sign said, "Door must be kept closed at all times by order of the fire department." He could never go out, for this would mean opening the door, which would violate the sign's command.

Alone on a bare wooden bench. Nothing to do. Nothing but to indulge in the human habit of contemplation. On his home planet, a rocky sphere that circled the star Omega Literalus, such contemplation was unheard of. All thought was directed toward a rationally determined set of goals.

The Literalist assumed that he would go insane. This was not surprising, since all humans were insane, at least so far as the beings of Omega Literalus understood sanity.

The Literalist had known, since being selected for the mission to earth, that his situation was precarious, that his lucidity would break down bit by bit. Only one other inhabitant of Omega Literalus had ever been sent to earth. Smuggled there as a small child, he had been unable to adapt, having lived on the edge of sanity and died young of broken health. This was the writer Franz Kafka, whose work the Literalist had studied to prepare for his mission on Earth.

Trapped. Trapped. The poor Literalist. There was only that one door, and no windows. Alone on a bench, unable to leave. Will he starve? Will his flesh rot and slough off leaving only shiny bones?

The Literalist remembered his subway ride this morning. He had sat paralyzed as the train snaked its way through the city and back, then begun the journey once again. "Doors will open on the left," the announcement had said, and they would open on the right, or "doors will open on the right" and they would open on the left. At first the Literalist had risen and attempted to leave each time, only to face an unopened door in front of a blank wall.

Then he had realized the paradox he was caught in: left and right were reversed. Of course, if he had chosen a seat facing the other direction he would not have faced this problem. But the fault was really the conductor's, who should have announced "Doors will open on the left"—or right, if that were the case—"relative to the direction the train is traveling," at each stop. Unless of course one were a fly the ceiling. But a fly wouldn't be able to understand the instructions, so the question was moot.

Finally, the Literalist had relaxed, used a deep-meditation technique to overcome his panic attack (such attacks are unknown on Omega Literalus), and reflected on his special training. To humans, everything is relative to a position assumed to be forward. Understanding this, the Literalist had been able to orient himself correctly and exit the train.

Later that day, the Literalist had waited in a long line. He was distraught, even though he knew it was a pointless feeling. Human emotions were overtaking him. Even in a short line, by the time he arrived he would lose his chance. After all, the coupon said "10% discount on future purchases." By the time he reached the checkout counter, it wouldn't be the future, but the present, and he would lose his discount.

Perhaps the humans who made the coupon had meant a purchase other than this one. But this, too, made no sense, since by the time that purchase was made it would, once again, no longer be the future.

The literalist thought back to his first night on earth. He had met a woman who had invited him to her room, and the Literalist knew that for earthlings this was considered good fortune. She had then asked him to sleep with her, which he knew was considered even better fortune.

So why had the woman been so upset when the Literalist had turned over on his side and attempted to sleep? Hadn't she asked him to sleep with her?

It was only later that the Literalist remembered his training. The difficult trip, together with the disorienting new environment, must have confused him. The explanation was so basic it was unbelievable that he hadn't understood it. Humans almost never say what they mean. What they mean could be completely the opposite, but more often it is related in only in some tangential way, or even completely unrelated. When the woman had said "sleep with," she had really meant "have sex with."

But wait, perhaps this disjunction was the key to the whole situation. The key to the door. But now the Literalist was thinking in metaphor, a sure sign that his entire mental state was deteriorating, that he was becoming human. Although at least there was a literal door here, even though the solution to his dilemma couldn't possibly be a literal key.

Perhaps this was another situation in which the sign meant something different than what it said. The Literalist remembered that the first step in solving such a puzzle is to figure out the reasoning underlying the sign (although often there are so many possibilities that simply contemplating them could drive one insane). The fire department was concerned with fires, and they were concerned with safety. The laundry room was full of machines that could catch fire. If the door were shut, the fire would be unable to spread.

So that was it! But as so often when dealing with earth, his momentary happiness turned instantly to panic. This was one of those rare instances in which human language actually means what it says. So he could not open the door. He was trapped. Trapped. Trapped.

Unless help came from somewhere. Unless help came from above. Unless help came from whom? From God? God? Now he understood. He understood why these poor, perplexed, helpless creatures, humans, limited in perspective by five puny senses, subject to the brutal drives of pain and emotion, believed in some mystic deity that, at the final hour, would save them. Would make everything all right.

The door opened with a burst of light!

"Marvin," said his mother. "Isn't the laundry done already? Another day gone. You've wasted another day without looking for a job."

The Mouse Chronicles

My tales of mice invading our lovely house, of mice fooling us time and again, of one especially bold mouse spirit reincarnated as a cat, must have come to the attention of the Great Guiding Mouse Spirit. I would have thought she would be pleased that her people—or should that be her creatures—were receiving some attention instead of just, as usual, being cursed at, trapped, and poisoned. Instead, the Great Guiding Mouse Spirit seemed angry; as if to retaliate for my stories, a mama mouse evidently gave birth in an obscure corner of our house, which was soon filled with the scamperings of adolescent mice, tiny creatures that darted along the edges in search of food or leapt boldly onto counters in the dark of night. In response, I purchased a variety of humane traps that catch mice without harming them, leading to frequent morning bike rides in the cold. (As hyper-environmentalists, my wife and I don't own a car.) The destination was a wide, tall-grassed meadow lined with trees. A perfect home for the little beings, perhaps? Or, in the coming winter, just a place to freeze to death? Still, mice were on this Earth for millions of years before humans arrived and should be able to survive the mild winters here in Maryland.

Perhaps the Great Guiding Mouse Spirit really was pleased with my little mice stories? Perhaps she is sending these mice as a tribute? From her perspective, aren't baby mice a holy gift? Or are they an inducement for me to write more mice stories, for more blasphemy? If this was her plan, it is working.

An Encounter

A mouse streaked across the floor in the early morning light. It seemed our catch-and-release traps weren't catching enough, and I would have to order something nastier. But I decided to double check the humane traps first, and indeed one of them had snapped shut. Inside, the mouse sat immobile, like a plastic toy gazing up.

After a quick bowl of oatmeal and a hot cup of mint green tea, I returned to the trap to see the mouse scurrying inside its plastic casing. I bundled in multiple layers and wrapped the trap into a plastic bag which I inserted into my black carrying-bag. Hopping onto my bike, I headed into the morning traffic, sticking mainly to the sidewalks and a hiker-biker path to avoid being flattened by some enormous truck (and to protect the tiny rodent under my care). The air was crisp and enlivening, not the frigid, windy blasts I had imagined. After crossing Gude Drive, I glided past a warehouse to a local meadow hidden in the rear.

It took a couple of tries to get the latch to release the door. The mouse whipped out, a bolt of energy—a tiny spark of being, the music of the universe surging through—and disappeared into the tall strands of grass.

I felt wise and benevolent having saved a life, however seemingly insignificant. I would say I felt humane, but humans are too often angry and violent, so "humane" is the wrong word. Maybe "animalane"?

I hope the mouse is happy. Perhaps it is already having children, plotting with them a return to our house to make mischief once again.

Conversation with a Mouse

Me — Dear mouse, I have captured you and am taking you to a nearby field only partly because I love every living thing (excluding cockroaches, viruses, Donald Trump, Vladimir Putin, perhaps rats, and a growing list of others), but also for pragmatic reasons—I fear poison, and am worried a poisoned mouse carcass could rot and smell, hidden in some obscure cupboard. Also, I don't want to set snap traps because I am worried that I will forget about them and eventually one will injure my wife, myself, or our wonderful cat, Thelma.

Mouse – You are a Nazi, purveyor of a ruthless extermination campaign against mice.

Me – That's unfair and hyperbolic. The Nazis are the greatest evil in history. They used systemic mass methods to trap, torture and kill their victims with guns and poison gas.

Mouse – Exactly what your entire species is doing to mice.

Me – Not true. We do it in as humane a way as possible. Or most of us. Or at least some of us. Plus, you mice can bring disease and make us sick. Plus, if you're left unchecked, you will just breed and undermine us in greater and greater numbers.

Mouse – All of these things were said about the Jews.

Me – But in the case of the Jews they were lies. In your case, sadly, they're true.

Mouse – We can't help it. Like you, we are just trying to survive. We take only a minute portion of your food, and almost always what you are otherwise wasting. If we occasionally bring disease, other humans also spread disease, yet you don't poison or kill them, or lock them outside.

Me – Actually, we sometimes do. Look at all the homeless humans.

Mouse – What does that say about you? It seems that we mice are the superior species. We've never had mice Nazis hunting and killing other groups of mice.

Me – Maybe, but I am different. Look, I am taking you to a nice field where you can live a good life. And there are others of us humans who don't eat meat, who don't harm other living animals.

Mouse – Thank you. But could you just leave me in your nice, warm house? I could die in the coming winter cold or be snatched by a hawk.

Me – The hawk needs to eat too. That would be a good end for you. Part of the balance of nature.

Mouse – It's easy for you to say that. You're not the one being eaten. If you really believe what you just said, you'll fly to Africa or Asia and sacrifice yourself to a lion. Part of the balance of nature.

At this point, we had arrived at the field. I removed the trap from my knapsack and opened it. The mouse sprang into the field, bolted away. I hope she writes to tell me of her daily progress. But I didn't leave my address, for fear she'd return.

At Home, Never Alone

The surge in mice was only the latest in a series of small invasions over our 15 years in the house, including mildew, cockroaches, and even more mildew and mold that eventually required a complete redoing of our front bathroom. Humans are continually fighting for a pristine environment free from the nature that we are part of, the plants and mold and microbes and scurrying creatures that want to share our habitations and, often, our food, even our bodies. Nature is a vicious war of all against all. Nature is a cycle, cruel but with a kind place for an enormous variety of species. We humans want to break that cycle, to utterly alter environments so they please us or serve our wishes, and often we have the means to do so.

Interlude

Reaching behind a chair to pick up a dropped piece of candy that had somehow rolled there, I lurched back with a start. A mouse! But wait, it was a stuffed mouse that my wife had bought for Thelma. Over the years we'd accumulated a mini-horde of fake mice, some plastic, one wooden, one brightly striped. Currently, I encountered a stuffed brown figure with shiny eyes. Perhaps these shamanistic mice idols were in part responsible for summoning the plague of actual mice?

Conversation with a Human

"You take your mice a whole mile away?" said my friend Anatolia on the phone, incredulous. "I used to just dump them into the yard."

"They can get back into the house if you do that."

"They probably did. I didn't think about that."

"Did you use humane traps to capture them?"

"Sticky traps. Mostly the mice were completely stuck and I'd throw them away, but a few the traps had just gotten by the back leg. I'd just toss them into the yard."

She must have had mountains of mice, a vast infestation. What had she done to upset the Great Guiding Mouse Spirit? What would the mouse with whom I had that wretched, yet somehow enlightening, conversation call her? Probably something horrible, which would be unfair. She is a kind and caring person. I'd say she wouldn't hurt a fly, but she obviously would. But she's thoughtful to other people.

They are just mice, after all. Their brains are small, their lives short and opportunistic.

A Brief Conversation with My Wife

"So many mice? How did we get so many?"

"It's a metaphor for Covid."

"Oh, the mice are just a metaphor. They'll be happy to know that."

The Great Guiding Mouse Spirit is very, very angry!

Infestation

My wife pointed out the brown pellets scattered among the counters where we keep culinary implements and some food. A quick internet check revealed that these were, indeed, mouse droppings. As a result, the whole morning was spent moving objects, scrubbing cooking and cake pans, containers, etc. The mice had ripped open a bag of popcorn and scattered it everywhere, and also torn through the bottom of a flour bag. A pile of napkins seemed okay, but perhaps had been contaminated. I used some of these to scrub down the counters and threw the whole pile out, along with a bunch of plastic forks and knives. Then I did a final scrub of the surfaces with disinfectant.

It was time to go toxic, as the humane mouse traps were failing to catch any more mice. Perhaps the remaining rodents had learned to avoid them? It was only a few days after my conversation with Anatolia, and I reluctantly followed her guidance and bought sticky traps. The very first day, I caught one mouse affixed to a sticky trap, a tiny thing whose body sat there like a stuffed mouse. I marveled at its intricate paws and whiskers.

As I tossed it into the trash, I said a short, silent prayer.

I Try New Tactics

Since cat food is the center of numerous mice festivals, I moved it to the family room at the back of the house, where it might attract fewer little mouths. On either side of the bowl, I placed a humane mouse trap, while a few feet away, under an end table, I hid a sticky trap with a blob of peanut butter in the center.

Bad News at My Doorstep

My wife saw on Nextdoor East Rockville that mice surges are happening in multiple houses. Perhaps it's the strange weather? Is it climate change related? Anatolia thinks it's because the epidemic means less trash outside, so the mice are finding their way into homes. In any case, we will likely experience more and more strange encounters with animals as humans continue to alter the environment. It's like in *Julius Caesar,* where all of nature is perverted by the Emperor's coming death, where owls hoot throughout the day, lions give birth on the streets, packs of mice hunt and eat cats. The divine balance is broken.

Only in current times such strange behavior is planetary wide and will persist for decades, likely the rest of human existence.

A Foolish Inspiration

"Maybe I'll design a cooperative game in which each player takes the part of a mouse just trying to survive," I tell my wife.

"Don't give yourself a nervous breakdown," she replies. "They're only mice."

I Learn about Mice from a Secondhand Source

My wife mentioned reading somewhere that house cats these days are less likely to stalk mice and more likely to befriend them. That makes sense, since nowadays cats get food from cans opened by humans, not from hunting and fending for themselves. Cats are true welfare cases, but one never hears Republicans complaining about them. In any case, Thelma was certainly blasé about the mice, happy to share her food with them. After all, aren't they fellow furry four-footed mammals with warm blood and adorable whiskers, with live births who nurse their young?

My wife also mentioned that mice are social, that mice in a leader position will try to rescue lesser mice. This explains why mice caught in a sticky trap squeal in such a pathetic manner, struggling to attract help.

Mass Casualties

Was that birds tweeting just outside the kitchen window, or a mouse squealing? I checked a sticky trap and it had, indeed, caught a tiny twitching figure. I felt too disheartened to throw it away immediately. Besides, the sticky traps are quite large. Why waste them, when they might catch more mice?

Poor creatures. They only want to live. But they are breeding like crazy, shitting on our counters, poisoning our food. In a horror movie, the creatures are evil, soulless, perhaps mechanical, or emanate from

Hell itself. But these mice are innocent and pure—mischievous, yes, implacable, yes, but innocent.

Innocent creatures who only want to live. That was my mistake, sympathizing with the first mouse who appeared. I waited for a whole month before buying the first humane traps, another month before the sticky traps. We could live with a few mice, I thought. Peaceful coexistence. We have coexisted with one or two before, but never whole families of mice. Once they start breeding, that's it! I'd never make the same mistake. After we'd obliterated this colony, the instant another mouse appeared, out would come an array of humane traps to vanquish the problem early. And if that didn't work, sticky traps would follow.

Throughout the day I hear twittering—is it birds, dying mice, my imagination? In the evening, my wife hears the squeaking. "It's pitiful," she says. "Isn't there a better way to get rid of the mice?"

Another Dystopian Epic

I begin work on a novel in which humans discover that mice are as intelligent as people. They just don't have hands to create things or the size to compete with humans and must resort to asymmetrical tactics.

Once they learn to communicate, humans and mice negotiate for who gets to use what material goods under what circumstances, designating who will occupy what territory. A system of treaties beginning at the local level, in thousands of locations, quickly becomes global. Some humans refuse to negotiate and continue to kill mice indiscriminately. Others sign but then break treaties, taking territory and goods previously ceded to mice. In three different countries, civil war breaks out over the status of mice. Piece by piece, the old all-out warfare between mice and humans returns, although, because each side understands the other better, it is more ferocious. Various pacifist groups try to stop the war against mice using passive resistance, while a scattering of eco-terrorist actions dominate the news. This results in the infiltration and arrest of pacifist and environmental groups around the planet, with numerous instances of torture.

I write only one sentence of this novel, then delete the document without having named it. Heading into the kitchen to wash the dishes, I discover that the counter by the sink is covered with mice turds.

I Take Extreme Measures

I spot two mice one day and another in the morning. My wife sees two in the same period of time. We discuss whether to buy poison and decide it's the only option left (short of calling the exterminator).

On Amazon, I order an eco-friendly mouse poison, guaranteed safe for pets and humans. The most virtuous of poisons!

Casualty Count

One snowy morning, I hoist a humane trap into my bag, a quivering mouse within. In addition, I scoop up a humane metal trap designed to catch multiple mice, but with a flaw—you can't look inside to see if it's caught any mice. I trudge a half mile through the chill, through the patchy snow and ice, depending on who's shoveled, what's melted, etc. I'm well bundled and comfortable, actually enjoying my morning walk. Approaching a little woods at the far side of Maryvale Park, I whisper to the mice to enjoy their new home. Opening the metal trap, I am shocked when three mice spring out, like toys from a jack-in-the-box, scampering down an embankment. Trudging home, I briefly wonder whether the mice will thrive in the little woods, or freeze in the winter cold, or find some nearby house to plague. At this point, I scarcely care.

"We've gotten rid of six mice in the last two days," I tell my wife. "That could be good news—maybe they're almost gone. Or it could be bad news—maybe there are more mice than ever so we're catching more."

Here is a list of mice we've caught over the past month, as best I can reconstruct it:

·Big, fat mouse caught in the last of the old snap-traps: 1

·Mice caught in our humane traps and released: 11

·Mice caught and killed in sticky traps: 3 or 4. But some sticky traps are missing, so it's possible they caught mice and we just haven't found them.

Total count: 15 +

This is at least as accurate as the lists the American military put out of enemies killed and captured during the Vietnam War. And perhaps just as futile.

A Skirmish

Late in the mouse wars, I amble into the family room one fine morning, a bowl of cereal and yoghurt in hand, to be greeted with a thumping. On the right, Thelma munches at her bowl, indifferent to the suffering, squealing creature just a few feet away, under an end table. Examining the trap, I see it's caught not one but two full-sized mice. Very efficient!

But why must they squeal and struggle so?

Based upon a friend's suggestion, I grab a plastic bag from the other room, scamper back, use it to pick up the mice, envelop them, and place them in the bottom of our freezer, the coldest part, atop a chunk of ice. There, I hope they will go into a deep hibernation. In a few hours, I'll toss them into our huge, outdoor trash can, their final resting place.

I have nothing against mice, am strangely fond of them. They just want to survive in this crazy, marvelous, cruel world.

I say a small prayer to the Great Guiding Mouse Spirit, perhaps similar to the way some indigenous people pray to the spirit of the deer they've just killed.

An Unexpected Breakthrough

As far as I can tell, the poison is not working. Or maybe it is and the mice are going outside to die? In any case, who wants poison around the house? I move the refrigerator and a couple of rolling carts, sweep the far corners of the kitchen with a broom, scooping up poison pellets and mouse droppings alike. In the far corner behind the refrigerator, behind a fallen tile, lurks a hole, tiny by human standards but a superhighway for mice. For the time being, I seal it with half a bottle of Elmers' glue and tape.

It takes only a day for the foaming sealant to arrive. I move the refrigerator once again, shake the can vigorously, spray, and get . . . nothing. After more violent shaking and another try the sealant spurts out in a foaming wave. Perhaps this will finally solve the mouse problem?

With the kitchen safe, I move the cat food back there, since more mice have plagued the family room lately.

War Is Over

The mice seem to have disappeared. Or have they? One morning, I think I smell mouse droppings in the kitchen. That evening, do I hear mice scampering behind the couch near the newly repositioned cat food?

I move the cat food back into the family room, since if it does end up attracting mice I'd rather they stay in the back of the house.

On two evenings, my wife thinks she hears the squealing of a mouse caught in a sticky trap. I carefully check all remaining sticky traps, come up empty. But is there another hidden somewhere that I've forgotten?

I Discover What May Be the Last Mouse

I hold up a trap, peer with awe through the plastic casing at a teeny mouse with its miniscule whiskers and tail. Adorable! And yet, somehow alien and implacable, with designs on me and my family.

Thelma is also adorable, with delightful whiskers, smooth soft fur, a long tail. Yet, when I look into her eyes she, too, is sometimes alien and unknowable, using us to provide food, to bask in warmth. Is that love or is it opportunism?

Other people, too, seem at times alien to me, drawn by the opportunity for exchange, economic and otherwise. At times, I am alien to myself. What do I want and why do I occupy this body?

When you a release a mouse into a waiting field, it is a lightning bolt of energy, designed to find food, create more energy, find more food, and breed, creating more mice. It's all about survival and propagation. That's a sad version of the meaning of life.

Silence

Somewhere, the Great Guiding Mouse Spirit presides at a lonely funeral for the mouse colony that had invaded our house. It's been over a week since we've last seen, heard, or smelled the critters. Just today, our Roomba pushed out, from underneath the couch, an old sticky trap with two desiccated little bodies.

Billions of mice in millions of families and colonies exist around this great globe. Yet the Great Guiding Mouse Spirit remembers this one small band that briefly thrived at 535 Virgin Lane, memorializes them in their unsuccessful struggle to survive, to thrive. Somehow, she knows the perfect prayer for them.

Meanwhile, my wife and I breathe easy in our clean, quiet, comfortable home.

Epilogue

Sixty-five million years ago, a mouse-like creature survived the meteor that wiped out the dinosaurs, a creature that is the ancestor of humans and mice alike. The mice and I are extremely distant cousins. Still, it's true that mice may make us humans sick, that if left unchecked they will breed and overflow and we will be forced to kill far more than if we'd removed them early. It is eternal war with the mice.

Meanwhile, we ourselves are breeding and over-consuming, spreading poisons, warming the planet, cutting forests, draining swamps, blowing the tops off mountains. Mice have been part of ecosystems for millions of years.

Is the face of the mouse, caught in a sticky trap, our own?

Alternatives

A Short Alternative History of Planet Earth

As Natasha Cohen—a Black, Jewish, lesbian, humpbacked, left-handed dwarf—lay on her deathbed, she pondered why all her life she had drunk only from the cup of bitterness. Forty-four years of struggle against insurmountable odds. Why had she even bothered fighting? From her early teens, she had known that there was no escape. She had been judged and pronounced guilty from the moment of birth. For Natasha Cohen, the years of being misunderstood and outcast had so worn on her that at age 44—for many an age of new beginnings—she had the withered appearance of a 90 year old, a shrunken creature with flesh folded upon itself, with twitching limbs. Twice in her life she had met Black Jews, and once, unbelievably, a lesbian humpback dwarf—Elizabeth—with whom she had had a fervid affair. A brief, golden period until Elizabeth had been hit by a Toys R Us semi-truck bearing Christmas gifts to all the children of the world. For Elizabeth, who had been a fervent Christian, this was the only Christmas present. Not quite crucified, she was reduced to a bloody splotch rended by a huge tire tread. Nothing resembling a human body remained for decent burial.

Had Elizabeth lived, would religion have come between her and Natasha? Would Natasha have found Jesus? Could happiness arrive for a pair of lesbian dwarfs? The chance to find out was squelched all too quickly. And as Natasha sank into her final sleep, she thanked God for bringing her death. She could sense death closing in on her, a mysterious figure shrouded in black. But wait, was this death, or some other spirit?

The spirit spoke up with a voice like velvet. "Natasha. I am your guardian spirit and never have I been handed a case as hard as yours. All your life you have been misunderstood by all groups of people. Spurned by those who should have been your friends. Due to the unique circumstances of your life, I have made an unusual request of the Most Holy Spirit, and the request has been granted. Even I was surprised at this, for it has been several thousand years since the Holy Spirit has intervened, even in the slightest, with the laws that rule this universe. Of course, time and space are an illusion, depending upon one's perspective, which, however, one has no capacity to change, making them not an illusion at all, but we won't go into that now. Why muddle up your head with paradoxes beyond your understanding?"

Natasha was too polite to point out that the spirit had already done so. After all it was her guardian spirit and had gone to special and unusual lengths for her, and it wouldn't do to be rude.

"The request is this," continued the spirit. "You may be granted one wish of your choice. In this wish you may even go so far as to violate the normal rules of time and space, since they are, after all, problematic. You may also make it a fairly complex wish, consisting of numerous phrases and clauses, compound verbs, etcetera. Although the wish must follow the standard rules of English grammar, if you do happen to violate them you will be permitted to rephrase."

So, the spirit was something of a pedant. Already faced with death, the ultimate test for any human being, Natasha now had to tangle with the intricacies of English grammar. But she collected herself and, somehow, the right words sprang to her lips. "Spirit, all my life I've been an outcast, misunderstood on every side. Even my own parents, who had prayed for a child, didn't know what to do with me when I arrived. But what I ask isn't for myself, but for the human race. For the whole history of cruelty and misunderstanding that have burdened our species. What I wish is that all the differences that have separated people—race and sexuality and physical disability—that all of these simply did not exist and have never existed."

"Surprisingly well stated," said the spirit. "I had thought we would have to go through several drafts to get your wish to come out right, but that will do nicely. I'll rush off to the Highest and Most Holy Spirit to take care of your request as quickly as possible."

The guardian spirit was gone, leaving a darkness. A calming, swirling darkness, a whirlpool of nothing and everything that sucked Natasha inward, inward . . . .

A gentle chirping of crickets gave way to birds. Was it two of everything? The creation? Or was humanity acting out its part in evolution? Watching the grand sweep of history—the new history in its earliest days—Natasha was unsure. True, the couple referred to themselves as Urgham and Urv, which sounded faintly like Adam and Eve, but perhaps these grunts were merely the easiest sounds to transform into language.

A softly rising sun streaked its way through splotches of clouds, a play of light bouncing upon a nearby stream, whose trickling music trilled in syncopated harmony with the birds. A new day dawning in this sheltered cove. The first man-woman and the first woman-man grunted and cooed love calls. For, in accordance with Natasha's wish, both were hermaphrodites, capable of impregnating and being impregnated. There was to be no patriarchal domination in the new order, no homosexuality if all humans were capable of acting out either gender role.

Pregnancy happened soon, with each of the couple's bellies swelling. Natasha smiled; her new race would be able to populate the globe quickly. For Urgham, the baby slid out with relatively little pain, and soon the wrinkled little being slept peacefully in her mother's arms.

Urv faced a longer pregnancy, and she screamed out as she gave birth, never before aware that such pain was possible. For her second baby, however, birth was easier. The stars seemed brighter than possible in those days, and Natasha long remembered one particular night, a full bright moon overhead, hovering protectively over a peaceful little scene, the last flames of a flickering fire, the first couple falling asleep each with a baby at her breast, another child lying curled at their feet. Better than the Christ child in the manger. Still, Natasha wondered, why did they deserve to have such a tranquil life when hers had been so horrendous?

Not surprisingly, squabbling soon entered this new world, at least among the children. But Natasha decided that this was normal—it made them seem more human. Gruggg, the eldest, was Urgham's favorite (Natasha thought of all these creatures as "her"), while Urv preferred Ingggg, the youngest, and loved to stroke and play with her. The smallest of the middle children, Blub, they would shriek at and order to dig for roots to supplement the more easily picked fruits, as well as the occasional grasshopper or squirrel caught by the aggressive Gruggg, who loved playful sport. To Natasha it was familiar and disconcerting, yet also, in a strange way, comforting. Wasn't this normal family life, the kind she had never had?

Tired of squatting double, digging in the dirt with the worms and primeval ants, Blub would often wander off alone, up the nearby craggy mountain. What did she do there? Climb and hunt and ramble? Sit and meditate? Worship strange gods? No one knew, nor did this first human family care; only Natasha wondered. Their curiosity was oriented to the pounding of stones and sharpening of sticks, the fashioning of rudimentary tools, the invention of new words for new items: earth, sky, worm, apple. Nouns had far outstripped verbs in their fecund variety. But of Blub, no one inquired.

A shock, a start. Screams and blood. The first murder? So soon, so soon. Inggg's blood, her broken little body. Above her a wailing, a weeping figure. Urv. She is stunned, she does not know what has happened. It is unbelievable. Tears and blood. An injured mother, Urv squats fondling Inggg as though she were alive, coating her dangling arms in her daughter's warm blood. And a murky figure, a shadow, slips away in the darkness. Blub. Gone forever. Too late to take back. An ominous cloud, a cloud of wrongness, hangs above. It should never have happened. And yet it has. Tears are followed by screaming and blame. Unable to watch the little family tear itself apart, Natasha hid herself in a massive cloud to hibernate.

Within the recesses of her slumbering spirit, Natasha felt a calling to awakeness. The sweet perfume of flower petals permeated the air, honied incense rising, bonfires newly lit. The world was youthful and energetic, the energy of the moon rising above, of thick clusters of newly brilliant stars staring upon the planet, of a spring breeze licking through the early night. Dance and jubilation and youthful love, an energy Natasha had experienced only fleetingly during her own dreary life. And the people danced and celebrated and called to the goddess. The goddess Natasha, whose emptiness was filled with their spirit, something coming from nothing. And why not, she thought, as she danced among the dancing flames, around which danced and sang the swaying crowd, stained with the bright reds and purples of berry juice, tasseled with feathers and loose-fitting skins stripped from animals that had died a natural death, hides that danced and shook with the rippling crowd. Wasn't she the founding mother of this new race? Wasn't it she who had first conceived of this new humanity, a vision that included its foibles and jealousies, but excluded the hatreds planted deep within the flesh? A new race, free from the destructiveness caused by differences in skin color and genitalia.

And what of that old race, she wondered briefly as the incense and the night wind carried her above the celebrating crowd. Where had they gone? To some other place? To nonexistence? To hell? Very well, she thought, let them all go to hell, let them burn there forever. It would be no worse than the pain inflicted upon her during her own lifetime. And the dancing and yelling of the drunken worshippers crescendoed, vibrating through the chilly night air. This new race was all that counted. She loved them. She loved them. And she smiled upon the figures, limbs intertwined, drunk on grog and orgasm, gently sleeping.

Soon new forms of worship came to Natasha's tribe, the Natashites, most of whom considered her as one among many gods, albeit the one with a special affinity for the tribe. They began to bring her small animals for sacrifice, eating of their flesh and leaving the bones for Natasha's benefit. Natasha had never been a vegetarian, and although she found this practice annoying, she also considered it relatively harmless. After all, didn't they need to cause a little pain, at least to the lowliest animals, to highlight their own enjoyment, to sanctify Natasha's worth?

Soon, the animal sacrifice grew in scope. A group of children dragged a squirrel to the altar for an unofficial sacrifice. Instead of just killing the creature, they poked its eyes out, then cut off its limbs one by one, finishing with its tail, and watched as it writhed, as it bled to death.

The third time the children set out on their task, they were discovered. They had added a new twist to their ritual; having piled twigs upon the squirming, amputated body, they were attempting to burn the creature to death, but, it being a damp and drippy day, could not get the flint to spark. Three young lovers strolling in the woods (there being no distinct sexes, loving sometimes took place in threes) happened upon this scene, and began shouting. The largest of the three approached and towered over the children, demanding an explanation. The shortest child, a mischievous tyke, answered with a squeaky voice, quick and breathless. Soon the adult's companions came round, and instead of scolding the children, helped to shelter the altar from the wind and created the spark that set the whole thing alight.

Squirrel torture and sacrifice was soon a regular part of the Natashite rituals and quickly gave way to the slaughter of sheep. And Natasha did feel a certain pride. In expressing gratitude to their sovereign-queen, whose wish had, after all, brought them and their history to life, shouldn't the full range of emotions be displayed? Besides laughter and lust, aren't terror and pain part of the spectrum of the human condition? Without suffering, can there truly be joy? And they did owe Natasha all aspects of their existence. So it seemed right, and pleasing, that they displayed these emotions in sacrifices to her.

Soon dissension came to the Natashites. A few believed that Natasha was the mother of all gods, and was made manifest in the earth and sky, never assuming human form. This sect further believed that animal sacrifice was a desecration of the holy spirit that Natasha had placed in all beings. Refusing the altar upon which the majority of the Natashites sacrificed, they chose a new altar, a great flat rock hidden within a forest clearing that lay at the foot of a mountain. The tinkling music of a mountain stream played nearby, reminding Natasha of the original fountain that had gurgled for the first humans in this new world. On the flat rock, worshippers placed pungent flowers and herbs with sensual smells and sang pretty melodies. Natasha luxuriated for a spell in the peaceful enclosure, meditating and drinking in the words of worship. Soon, however, she realized that she was bored. She missed the whelping emotion of her other worshippers and hurried to join them.

She bounced upon cold gusts of wind, frenzied little gusts that carried her through the darkening sky, dark with thick clouds and the approach of night. A frenzied chorus of screams beckoned from below, yelps and bellows, a thickening disharmonious hullabaloo. The excitement crested as she approached the jubilant worshippers, who summoned her to their shrine. A large dark figure clothed in black garments led the proceedings, a faceless figure, a high priest who bellowed out words of praise to Natasha. And the chorus answered, lust answering lust in crescendoing waves. Tonight's sacrifice was to be a large animal, and Natasha could feel the rapid, warm pulse beating through the crowd. The night sky flashed yellow and rumbled with thunder, joining the rumbling mob.

And the crowd parted like a great sea and brought forth a figure bound and bowed. They pulled her forward and, with a start that Natasha would not have believed possible in her current wraithlike form, she realized that it was no animal. Or rather a human animal, struggling in terror. A silence fell, and the priest uttered incantations in a loud yet somehow flat voice, emptied of emotion as though aware of the enormity of what was to come. "The unbelievers have snuck away," he said, "and are even now performing their blasphemous rites. Yet we have caught one of their number and offer her. The ultimate sacrifice to the great Natasha." For her? Suddenly, aware of what was happening, the crowd grew silent as though they no longer believed in this event. Towering over the wriggling little body, the priest uttered some final syllables of worship, then raised high a slender, shining implement. A plunging dagger, a muffled scream, a final surge of fear and pain. For Natasha? True she was great, was the mother of this world, but did she deserve all of this? She felt both horrified and flattered. And uncertainty filled the night. Lightening flashed dimly in the distance, and those with keen ears heard a muffled thunder. The storm was moving away.

Searching through time and eternity. Two huge intersecting elements, riddles wrapped in mysteries, mazes within mazes. Natasha was lost.

What to do? Stand still, call for help? Mentally she called out again and again, thoughts echoing through her disembodied spirit, but she felt enclosed, alone. Could she be heard by any outside being?

Yes. The spirit had heard. The spirit was here.

"Oh Great Spirit," Natasha began.

"Not so great," said the spirit. "Let's have none of that overblown mumbo-jumbo."

"Oh Spirit, then."

"Yes."

"You seem to have pulled out of our initial bargain. Didn't I request an end to discrimination in this new world? And isn't this religious discrimination?"

"You requested, and I quote," said the spirit, popping out a scroll on which her original words were inscribed, "that 'all the differences that have separated people—race and sexuality and physical disability— that all of these simply did not exist, and had never existed.' Nowhere did you mention religion."

"Oh, so you're applying the letter of the law, but not the spirit."

"I am the Spirit of the Letter."

"The Letter? And do you mean also of the Word."

"The Word? No, no, that is a higher power than I. The Letter as in the kind of letter that delivers a message. For you see, I am only a messenger."

"Oh. Now I'm all mixed up and have lost my train of thought. My point is that by 'race and sexuality and physical disability' I was merely giving examples of various kinds of differences, differences being the main category."

"Ah, it's all in the syntax. Is that what you're getting at? Don't you think that we in the higher world, or lower world, or parallel world, depending upon one's point of view, already know this?"

"I'm not trying to get entangled in syntax. I'm no lawyer. I just want a world free of discrimination."

"So you wish for a race of insectoid creatures with no differences? A hive-like entity? Or a race of super-robots?"

"No, that's not what I meant at all. You're deliberately misinterpreting whatever I say. It seems as though you like to cause trouble. You should act according to my original intent."

"Original intent? But you yourself were not sure what you meant when you spoke those words."

"I thought I was."

"Thoughts are deceiving. Words never quite mean what they first seem to mean. And the further from their original utterance, the more this is true. So we have been letting you serve as a kind of barometer. You decide the shape and direction of your new world. You have been doing so all along."

"Then I renounce my role."

"You cannot do so. For you see a barometer has no will of its own. It merely reflects the movement of external elements, just as you reflect the changing circumstances of this new world."

Natasha meant to protest but was struck dumb. As she considered what to say she realized that the Spirit was gone, that she was alone once again.

A scattering. A replenishing. A spreading. The human race, eating of the fruits of the trees, of the roots of the ground, itself fruitful and multiplying. Struggling and dying. Stalking and being stalked by the other creatures that share the planet. Stalking and being stalked by its own members. Receding and licking its wounds, then replenishing and moving onward. A slowly changing mosaic. Tribal creatures that divide into difference. Was it this, Natasha wondered, that drove the human race, drove them to explore new geographies, to create new inventions? Could they not live in peace, nurturing each other, nurturing a love of learning and exploration? Was there something fatally wrong with her wish? Or with the nature of humanity? Or of the universe?

Orgies and drunkenness. Roasted goat and sheep flesh in rich sauces flavored by pungent spices from distant lands. A city besotted with grog and wine, with opium leaves refined and rolled, inhaled and exhaled from enormous hookahs decorated with intricate gargoyle carvings. Massages with fruit juices and oils. Swapping of wives and mistresses. Oral and anal, three way and four way sex in all manner of positions, with adults and, increasingly, with children. Such was the life of Goooduhmmmm, more than a city a product of empire, a leisure class with time to spare. In the distant reaches of the empire, sinewy slaves labored to provide the material goods—gold and incense, chariots and statues, spices and ointments—required by the people of Gooduhmmmm. Closer at hand, fatter slaves labored in the kitchens, baked and roasted, swept and organized and cleaned and, after each orgy, cleaned once again, picking up chicken bones and shattered pottery, scrubbing away splotches of vomit and semen. Occasionally a slave was punished for disobedience, a sacrificial victim of the frenzied group, raped from all directions, disfigured and burned.

The screams filled Natasha with a wild energy as she drifted, dispersed, through the smoke, through the wind currents, that flowed through Goooduhmmmm. On a hot, still day she would linger there, stagnant among the people who lay lazy and dizzy in the hot sun, still faintly nauseous from the latest orgy. What kept them going was the knowledge that another orgy was coming soon, another day of lust and passion. Still even these were becoming dull, leading to greater and greater extremes: more drugs, more sexual experimentation, innovative methods of torture. And Natasha had learned not to resist. As a goddess, she enjoyed being revered and feared. She ruled not just through love but through terror. The full range of passion. And these pathetic beings of clay, doomed to die. Doomed to put on passion plays, love and betrayal, endless reenactments, new versions of Romeo and Juliet, of King Lear, dramas that meant everything to the players, nothing in the vastness of time. On good old Earth Shakespeare had had it right. And Natasha saw how ephemeral these creatures were. One would die and two new ones would arise. They existed for her pleasure.

She wondered if she had been put upon the previous planet Earth, made to live her wretched life, by a god as bitter as she.

Natasha glanced again over the great panorama of the new world. The same. It was all the same. Freshly populated with peoples swelling and multiplying, multitudes of languages spilling from their lips, each with individual ways of expressing themselves, with ingenious arts, innumerable means of combining stones, woods, metals, dyes and unusual substances, into sculpture and painting. There were art forms undreamt of upon the old Earth, based on shifting combinations of smells, tastes, and touches. There were the Jumpabumpers, an athletic people who dwelt in the sweaty tropics, proud of their pungent aroma. They equated nobility with pungency; the stronger the smell emitted from their yawning pores the better the person. "A rich soul emits a rich aroma," was a common saying among them. Every year they held a great festival, with competition among the youth who had reached 14 years old, in wrestling, running, and climbing of trees, followed by a torturous march through thick jungles. Those who fell and broke a bone were judged unworthy of Jumpabumpian society and left behind. Each year at least one was ripped to death by a doglike pack animal common in those parts. Finally, those who returned were subject to a great contest of smells, judged on the saltiness and pungency of their stench and given a thumbs up or thumbs down by the tribal elders. The latter were immediately stoned to death. While farting could increase one's chances of surviving, it could not make up for a total lack of sweatiness.

Then there were the Frigglefrippfropperrs, who spoke in high squeaky voices, whose language was a series of buzzes, squeaks, and beeps. They took pride in the volatility of their speech. The higher the pitch the better. Those with particularly sharp, frenetic voices were made nobles, while those with low, dull voices were considered inferior, cast out from the majority. The lowest of all were made to wear ugly rags, their faces disfigured, forced to carry before them buckets of human excrement, so that they would offend every sense of the ordinary Frigglefrippopperrian, who would know to keep away.

Natasha witnessed also a great tribal war between the Muthaluvvs and Luvvamuths, who had once been blood sisters but who now killed each other upon sight. Those unlucky enough to be captured would be tortured, forced to renounce their religion and killed upon confession of their crimes. The reason for this feud is that the two tribes differed in their worship of Natasha. At religious feasts both ate the great Muk Ostrich egg, which symbolized, in its fertility, roundness and completeness, the primal cycles of life. The Muthaluvvs, however, cracked these eggs with the skinny side pointed upwards to the heavens, symbolizing life-giving and the vast mystery of Natasha. The practice of the Luvvamuths was utterly different: they pointed their eggs to the ground, giver of fertility and life, as they cracked them and shouted holy incantations. Cracked. Neither the Muthaluv nor the Luvvamuths could understand ground and sky as united.

Lost among the clouds. In rough outline, Natasha saw the future of this new world, and it resembled the old. There would be wars, oppression, weapons of mass destruction, genocide. The same old same old. What a wretched species this humanity, in whatever guise. Would it blunder its way to a better future? She did not care to find out.

Returning to the Guardian Spirit, Natasha demanded to be thrown into the void.

"You have already been granted your wish for a new world," said the Spirit, "and this is a great privilege, beyond what anyone else has ever received. Now you must live with the consequences."

"It was presented under false pretenses. You offered it as a gift, and it turned out to be a curse."

"Isn't that always the way it is with wishes? You haven't studied your fairy tales very well."

"Look at the gravity of this situation. My deathbed. I was sick and depressed. You haven't taken this into account. It wasn't a fair bargain, fairly offered."

"Oh, so you want fairness? You could have wished for the void at that time. Eternal nothingness. Eternal tranquility. Ignorance is bliss. Do you want me to destroy this new world?"

"No, that would be unfair. Unless the creatures living there agree to it."

"You know that they never will. And I can't send you into the abyss without destroying this world."

"Why not? Aren't I just one of many gods?"

"You are and you aren't."

"Where does talking in paradoxes get us?"

"You are the prime mover, the dream weaver."

"So is the new world just a dream."

"Yes, but so was the old. So are they all."

"So why does it matter?"

"A dream with the terrible force of reality."

"How melodramatic. You disgust me. If you were my lover, I'd leave you."

"But now I will leave you. Or rather send you away . . . ." And with that the spirit began to shrink and spin, like a sock lost in a laundromat or a toy boat in a draining bathtub, or a cockroach in a toilet, spinning as it is flushed away. Centrifugal force. Natasha felt herself propelled, splitting up, dispersing. There was no longer a Natasha, but a billion sparks, a billion souls, or perhaps a hundred billion, souls that were and would be dreamlike and filled with terrible reality, living out a history that Natasha had initiated without understanding. Now there was no Natasha, but no void either, or rather a great black void and within it a bubble of life, a bubble blue with oxygen and hydrogen, seething with life like some plague, a plague of lonely, separate souls bound together on this vast and complex planet, playing out a new history, the same old history, wondrous and terrible.

The Practical Importance of Certain Philosophical Questions

Cal, a short heavy man in a business suit, was carrying chunks of lava. Once seething with fiery life, these chunks were cold and dormant, capable only of dragging down their bearer. Heat and pressure were now the province of Cal; sweat spewed from the little holes which peppered his flesh, just as the lava had once spewed from a gaping crater.

In the distance, rising behind a series of barren foothills, stood a brown volcano. However, this was not the volcano from which Cal's lava had originated. Cal's lava was imported from far-off lands, carried by teams of struggling mules (which, however, had not struggled as hard as Cal). Other lava chunks, from other volcanos, lay in a heap in a nearby field.

The sun rose and Cal, dripping with sweat to ward off the heat, carried lava. The sun set and Cal slept and the sun rose and Cal carried lava. Each day was the same, with the exception that the sun seemed imperceptibly hotter. Time marched in a different rhythm with Cal so busy. In younger days he had been lazy, lying about, drinking in the world with his senses, gazing up at the puffy floating clouds and the vast sphere of the sky, turning his head to where his eyes kissed the equally vast horizon. Or he contemplated nearer objects, rocks and grass speckling the ground echoing the patterns of the overhead clouds, or ants disturbing the peaceful groundscape, marching with fervent purpose. Now, like the ants, Cal was engaged in an important task.

One day Al, a man without a business suit, with a shaggy face a bit too young and round for a full beard, came walking by. He did not notice Cal. He was looking at the sky, or perhaps at a lumbering bumblebee.

Crash!

"See here, young man," said Cal, "why don't you watch where you're going? You made me drop my lava."

"Sorry," said Al in a blank kind of voice, and he strolled on, following the sky. Cal continued at his labor, stooping to gather the fallen lava.

But as Al walked, a wrinkle formed on his smooth forehead, followed by the creeping of a second wrinkle. A thought, perhaps slipping in through these new-found wrinkles, came to him. He turned and, with newfound purpose, marched toward Cal.

"Tell me," he asked, "why are you gathering these stones?"

"They are lava. I must spread them everywhere, filling the cracks and crannies around this valley."

"But why?"

"You see that volcano? Many thousands of years ago it erupted in torrents of fire, blotting out all surrounding life. Gradually the lava cooled into black rock. Still more gradually it cracked and crumbled away. Now it is vanished, either dispersed or faded into the soil."

"So?"

"Look here, young man!" Cal's arms sprang upward like a marionette's. The lava they had held crashed, once again, onto the ground. "Look here. Suppose a man, let us call him X, visits this valley some time in the future. He will see this lava. He will say, 'Aha, there was once an eruption here.' And he will be right."

"I see," said Al. In the distance, a vulture cut the sky and disappeared beneath the horizon. Like the vulture, Al wondered what could be behind this horizon. So he sauntered onward.

But once again something happened. Perhaps a minor angel escaped from the heavens (or someplace lower) and whispered questions into

Al's ear. He could not avoid glancing back. And having glanced back he was, once again, compelled to turn back.

"What is it?" Cal snapped when he saw Al return.

"I'm still confused. I know that X will have the right answer. Still, something seems wrong."

The air rumbled.

"Because even though X knows about the eruption, he doesn't know why he knows. He thinks that the lava he sees comes from this volcano and therefore concludes that it must have erupted at some time in the past. But his conclusion is based upon a false premise. Indeed, he might conclude that the volcano erupted more recently than he thought."

"Silly boy," cried Cal, exasperated. "That's the whole point of this project—to show the difference between knowledge based on truth and knowledge based on falsehood. More than that, it's to question the whole idea of knowledge. To build a lasting testament to the permeability of rationality, of empirical belief . . . ."

The volcano's red-hot belly blasted outward, upward, over the hills, and into the valley. Strands of flame, molten liquid, smoke, streams of death, shot over the valley smothering Cal and Al. They had time to glance up, but that was all.

Corn

What had we smoked at Jasmine's party that night in Hell's Kitchen? Some herb from the exotic far east? Unthinkingly, we sucked it in greedily from an enormous communal hookah. Tasting of pungent cinnamon, it filled the lungs and danced through the veins, until one's skin tingled and vigorous dots swam, like psychedelic sperm, before one's eyes. Even Bob, that strange visitor from Indiana who had refused every drink all night, had refused even one hit of a marijuana cigarette, had taken a sample puff from the hookah, although he had quickly given up in a flurry of coughing.

Bob looked the part of a Hoosier, a large, hammy figure. A plaid red shirt stuck out from his baggy overalls, while the stereotypical straw hat was planted firmly upon his head. A few of us wondered, briefly, who he was, what he was doing here, who had invited him. But all kinds of people passed through Jasmine's parties, some even stranger than Bob, so we quickly forgot about him and enjoyed the festivities. At first the music had been too loud for conversation, but by late in the evening only the soft tinkling of a piano remained, while the few remaining guests talked softly or nodded off on the silken cushions that graced Jasmine's apartment. Most had paired up with someone of the opposite sex (or a few of the same sex, or of indeterminate sex) and we lay in each others' arms softly stroking, speaking softly. Except, unusually, for Jasmine, who for the first time anyone could remember remained alone. And except for Bob who, like some ineffectual Hoosier scarecrow, had faded into the background, so that it seemed unclear as to whether he even knew how to talk.

Finally, Jasmine danced over to Bob, shook her breasts at him three times, gave him a soft kiss, and spoke. "Most of us are scared to cross the Hudson," she said in a voice that teased like the ringing of Christmas bells. "Some don't even believe there is life outside of Manhattan, although most have visited the outer boroughs, and some have made it as far north as the Catskills. A few have ventured as far across the Hudson as Hoboken. Of course, many of us have hopped on a plane to California, and the hardiest, bravest adventurers have even made it to such fabled lands as Nevada and Arizona. But between East and West there seems to lie nothing except the Midwest. Tell us about Indiana."

Bob spoke in a slow, strange language which some of us recognized as English. "There is one feature," he said, "which determines all life in Indiana, and that is corn. Fish live in oceans, birds in air, and Hoosiers in corn. It is their sea. Yet fish have more to do, more to experience, than Hoosiers. Fish can maneuver up and down, can dart among the coral, can evade larger fish, can enjoy viewing, and eating, great schools of smaller fish, in many colors and shapes. Hoosiers are more like nomads in the desert, moving endlessly across a flat, never-changing landscape. The corn is everywhere, in rows, stretching its arms to the sky, each stalk calling to God."

We sat there mesmerized by Bob's languid drawl. While he spoke more slowly than a New Yorker could even imagine, he was, somehow, impossible to interrupt.

"Only the corn convenes with the heavens. The people are bound to the endless rows of corn, which form paths, straight and narrow. Every day the people trod down these paths, beginning when the sun first glints over the horizon, following its passage through the vast sky, until it descends, a huge bloody sphere, beneath the horizon.

"Hoosiers are a solitary, silent lot. They trudge forward all day through the corn stalks, peering only ahead, plucking an ear here, an ear there, shucking them skillfully with one hand and flinging the husks to the ground. To the rhythm of their walking, they munch upon the sweet kernels, row by row yet somewhat unevenly. There is nothing like fresh Indiana corn, sweet and delicious, bursting with energy poured from the sun's sweet rays. In school you have probably been taught the virtues of a balanced diet, of the food pyramid, but this concept does not apply to Hoosier corn, for its goodness swells with all vitamins and minerals, everything one needs to build strong teeth and bones, firm muscles, well-oiled digestive systems, keen vision and hearing. For this reason, nobody is as healthy as a Hoosier, a naturally tough breed anyway, although they do tend toward pot bellies. Corn is fattening when eaten in large quantities.

"Does this mean that the solution to famine in impoverished countries, to rows and rows of sad eyes, of starving children, lies in the Midwestern heartland, in the perfect nutritional balance of the endless fields of corn? I confess, most Hoosiers haven't thought about such questions but, being something of a philosopher, I have considered it at great length. And alas, I have concluded, the answer is no, for it is an established fact that this corn is best under the brilliant Hoosier sun, in the fresh Hoosier air, freshly plucked and eaten. To corn, Indiana is the center of the universe. Just as our planet depends upon a mother sun for its very being and this same sun once existed as a puny part of a vast cosmic mass, so corn vibrates with goodness only in its homeland. As a tender stalk of corn moves further from Indiana, it slowly loses its taste. All vitality is sapped from it, all healthfulness, until it is a limp, tasteless, drooping shell, a shibboleth of its former self.

"Because of his access to fresh corn, the native Hoosier is one of the luckiest beings in the universe. Yet also one of the loneliest. Hoosiers never travel in groups, and this I cannot explain. Perhaps it is because economic necessity which, under ordinary conditions, forces humans to band together, is inapplicable under the unique circumstances of Indiana. That which we think of as holding us together, friendship and laughter, is weaker than the annoyances, the petty misunderstandings, the clashing of egos, which inevitably occur between people. Under the perfect conditions of Hoosier life, it is possible for people to live alone, and so they do. This at least is one explanation for the solitary nature of life in

Indiana. It may just be, however, that the people are different from those elsewhere, of a particularly strange and taciturn breed.

"There is, of course, one purpose for which we Hoosiers cannot remain alone. This is procreation. Following the laws of nature, that a population expands to the limits of the environment which contains it, one would expect a swelling, overpopulated state which eventually depleted the corn, however vast its extent. This is not the case, for in Indiana the population is so small, and the acreage of corn so vast, that it is a rare occasion when the paths of two individuals cross. That both should be young enough to breed, and that one should be male and the other female, is a cause of great excitement. It is only such a chance meeting that distinguishes one day from another, bringing the elements of time and change into lives otherwise as placid and unchanging as the ocean waves, or as the ceaseless waves of Hoosier corn. And, just as corn is pollinated by bees working tirelessly to maintain the balance of nature, so the meeting and mating of a Hoosier couple occurs just enough to perfectly maintain the population, perhaps twice in the lifetime of a typical specimen.

"The offspring of this fleeting romance are little trouble. Due to the corn's healthful qualities, the pregnancy is free of discomfort; when the baby does arrive, it glides painlessly from the mother's womb. The little tyke, perfect in every feature, needs care for only a few short months. The mother cradles the darling thing in her arms, rocking it tenderly. When it cries, she suckles it gently to her breast and soothes it to sleep. Soon enough it starts to crawl. Once this happens it is no longer a burden of any sort; the mother merely sends it down an alley of corn, like a bowler releasing a ball, where it crawls straight and true, surviving on the smaller stalks of corn which nestle close to the ground. So is the Hoosier baby weaned.

"And what of the couple whose union created this baby? Is there no great passion between them? After their act of love, as darkness hovers above, they lie side by side, hand in hand, under the blanket of night, and stare up at the vast heavens. The stars burst out, more brilliant than elsewhere on earth, filling the sky with diamonds of light. The constellations are visible: centaurs gallop across the sky, crabs crawl, gods frolic. The seas and skies and deserts intermingle, swelling with beauty. And the couple gazes at the heavens, arm in arm, their minds wandering until sleep overtakes them, bringing dreams of the fluxing constellations and the spiral of the Milky Way, which circles even beneath their closed eyelids. . . ."

At this moment Bob was interrupted by an ugly snore. It was Jasmine, who had fallen asleep. Her mouth was flung open, a gaping, distorted hole. Bob grew silent, and as my eyelids shut, I felt myself falling into the cavern of Jasmine's mouth, into a land of surreal dreams.

One Man's Trash

As I emptied the trash, I noticed that a trove of glasses had been slipped into the garbage bag's gaping mouth. "Hey," I asked my wife, "have you thrown out my old glasses"?

"They were just sitting in a heap," she said. "Some of them must have been decades old." It was true, I had left them beneath my nightstand indefinitely. Still, just tossing them out was wasteful. There were kids in third world countries who could use them. Of course, "third world" is no longer acceptable, as it can be seen as lesser; "developing nations" is now the preferred designation. But some of them never seem to develop, so is it really accurate to call them "developing"? As so often happens, I had become lost in thought, paralyzed. If I wanted to restore the glasses, I had better act now.

I dove into the garbage bag's vast mouth, pulled like a tiny spaceship into a black hole on my quest to restore vision to distant corners of planet Earth. (Though if Earth is round, can it have corners? All metaphors fail, most sooner than later, though since we think in metaphors, since language itself is a kind of metaphor, we have no choice but to use them). I was adrift in a vast sea of waste—or was it an ocean, a galaxy, or even a multiverse—again with the metaphors! My associative thinking often keeps me from accomplishing much of anything.

Back to the universe—or whatever—inside the garbage bag, through which I swam in a primitive doggie paddle style. I never did master more sophisticated strokes that require you to turn your head to breath. Banana peels and apple cores drifted by, along with a huge, stinking squash rind that had been part of yesterday's dinner. Should I not have composted them? An enormous, empty Amazon box bumped into my forehead—it had so recently been filled with sweet expectation. Should

I not have recycled it? Still, we are a society built on waste, and it seems impossible to avoid creating vast troves of trash as part of the great American consumption machine. It's all so overwhelming. And where were those glasses?

In the kingdom of the legally blind, is she with glasses Queen? If I did succeed in my quest to recover this jumble of glasses and have them delivered to the yearning masses overseas, would I be endowing myself with a kind of kingship among the recipients? Would I be an emperor, and if so was this quest as much about my imperialist need to put a stamp on the planet as about compassion for others? Perhaps I was simply a condescending benefactor trying to buy cheap absolution for my guilt at being born among the lucky ones. Most likely, the recipients would soon take the magical glasses that restored their vision for granted, would expect more, would become entitled, the ungrateful bastards!

Getting nowhere fast and slow, I tried switching to the breaststroke, which was somewhat better. I swam through ghosts of trash past, a smart phone recently discarded, a Roomba, power cords beyond counting for God-knows-what devices. Fortunately, none of the larger items had been tossed into the trash bag. It could have been deadly to run into our last washer-dryer, a lemon that had needed multiple repairs before we discarded it after only two years. Made cheap in China, it had been easier to replace than repair. Who cared about the sweat and tears of the Chinese workers? Besides, they needed the employment—for them, it was an opportunity.

And now I came upon older trash—a flip phone. A netbook. A Magnavox Videowriter, my first word processor. Stuff no one under thirty even remembered. Had all this gone into the very same trash bag? Perhaps this vast bag was itself a metaphor or a dream? But no, it felt as real as the living, breathing smart phone in my breast pocket, the heartbeat that kept me connected to reality.

I decided I'd better call my wife and explain to her my whereabouts. But all I got was an error message explaining that I was out of service range.

I must be miles beyond those lost glasses by now. They scarcely seemed worth it. Perhaps this would turn into a quest for home, an insignificant version of *The Odyssey*. Could I ever find my way back through this wilderness of trash?

But no, I was already home. We Americans literally are what we buy, and this was a record of my past, of who I was. I would learn to enjoy it, to luxuriate, not in the new and trendy, but my whole history of consumption.

So here I float, happily meditative among oceans of not trash, but fine consumer goods. I have attained a kind of Nirvana. I do not need glasses. For the first time in my life, I have 20 20 vision.

Five Difficult Tasks

One dawn an angel (or perhaps a devil) came to me with five tasks. Though the angel was a creature of myth, she appeared more real than reality, every part of her swirling with life, colors so sharp as to blind, a face everchanging: a griffin; a medusa; a sphinx; Nut, Egyptian goddess of the sky sowing seeds upon the Nile; Sita, Ram's faithful wife turned vengeful because the people had betrayed her; the Virgin Mary; Khadija bint Khuwaylid, Mohammed's first follower and the first of 13 wives; Mystery: the Great Whore of Babylon. To say this angel was a creature of the Word would probably be a lie; rather, she seemed a creature of far more than the Word; indeed, even to call her an angel is problematic. Perhaps to even tell this story is a desecration.

I felt myself incapable of performing even one task, but the angel, devil that she was, brought me five.

The first task, to end poverty on Earth, was simply impossible, so I pleaded with the angel to reduce it. To my surprise, she quickly gave way, and altered the task to merely shoveling the snow upon the walk, so that no one would slip. I joyfully accepted this, for I had shoveled snow often as a child, at times with great glee, although more often whiny and resistant. I grabbed a huge shovel and began, with enormous energy, to scoop up mounds of snow, casting them with abandon to one side or other, piling mountains that dwarfed me, stretched to the sky. The weather was surprisingly warm and I sang as I worked, songs of praise to the great blue sky and the morning sun, which rose above, and glinted off, the snowy mountain peaks on either side.

Soon enough, though, I stopped singing, bored. Shovelful after shovelful after shovelful. I began thinking of motion studies and wondered if there were a quicker, more efficient way to work. My mind drifted to my little brother, how when we used to shovel the walkway I had thrown snowballs and made him do more than his share. Tormenting him had made shoveling fun; now, in my alone-ness, the endless white landscape tormented me. Crystal flakes of snow, almost large enough to view their intricate patterns, drifted and swirled sporadically down, making my task endlessly harder. The walkway seemed longer with every shovelful; as I gazed down its length, I could see no end. Worse, the temperature had slowly been dropping and bitter cold fought through my coat, through my shirt, gripping at my skin so that my nerves tingled. My back ached. My nasal passages filled with mucous, until a great fit of coughing phlegm forced me to stop. I began again, but my stuffed nasal passaged soon paralyzed my heaving lungs. I stopped again and, gasping, blew two huge streaks of vapid yellow snot, which bore holes into the piles of snow. I blew and blew, melting the snow around me. Finally, lungs clear, revitalized, I began shoveling with new vigor, pure determination. Growing tired again, I sank to my aching knees, somehow rose, kept at it. Finally, I reached the street, which had been cleared of snow. In the distance, I spotted the rear of a huge yellow plow continuing on its job. However, mine was finished. A long black limousine pulled up the freshly cleared avenue. Inside the angel, sporting a huge pair of pointy pink glasses, lounged behind the wheel.

"Excellent job," she said as I hopped into the car. "Of course, anyone can fulfill a physical task. Let's test your intellect a bit. It would be too much to ask you to learn all the wisdom of human history. Since I'm a soft-hearted sort, I'll be content with the whole of English history, literature, and philosophy. But no, even that's too much. Let's just say, the whole body of Shakespeare's work. Rather politically incorrect, a dead white male and all, but you have to start somewhere."

The new assignment filled me with joy. I was familiar with *Macbeth, Romeo and Juliet, The Tempest, Hamlet,* of course, and a few of the historical plays, and I felt sure I could master the others. The angel drove a twisty road up a high mountain to a monastery at the very peak that seemed to teeter as if threatening to fall into the clouds. Inside the stone arches were sunny gardens with swinging chairs. It seemed a delightful place to study! The angel showed me to the library, which was a disappointment—gray and gloomy with a single reading lamp that cast a dim beam. The volumes that lined the bookshelves smelled of mildew. When I saw *The Complete Shakespeare,* though, it gave me hope. It was large, but relatively compact. "I can master this," I thought.

I decided to read through in order and was generally disappointed. The introductions explained that most were taken either from history or from old tales. "This guy couldn't even come up with his own plots," I thought. Worse, they were full of bad puns. "Why, I'm more clever than the Bard," I mused to myself. The plots were contrived, with unbelievable masquerades, switching of sexes and identities that didn't seem adequate to fool anyone, with hopelessly contrived endings in which everything came out fine for no apparent reason. I had studied the *deux ex machina* in Freshman English and Shakespeare seemed to use it endlessly. "Is this the best that was ever thought and felt and lived and written," I pondered incredulously.

But there was still the matter of the other volumes in the library. I glanced through and they were all *about* Shakespeare—his life, his times, his sonnets, most of all his plays. Endless analysis from interminable perspectives—historical, biographical, psychoanalytic, existentialist, deconstructive, feminist, Freudian. What horde of miserable bookworms would write so many volumes about one man? Some of them appeared beat up and thumbed through, but most looked as though they'd barely been opened. Still, I'd better work my way through them— perhaps they'd illuminate all the fuss about this Shakespeare fellow.

These books proved both more interesting and more boring than I had expected. More boring when they merely summarized the plays, or explained their meaning in an obvious way, or fell into using obtuse jargon. These I would fling aside in an ever-growing pile—"useless detritus," I would think as I lofted the book scornfully into the air. The volumes that proved interesting were those that had less to do with the plays themselves. Shakespeare's life fascinated me: the impetuous, unknown schoolboy who matures into a figure of genius. The only problem was that he was dead before his fame reached its absolute height, which seemed terribly unfair to me.

The history of England, too, unfolded itself in these volumes as a rich theater, richer, it seemed, than that which took place in the smaller world of the Globe theater. The psychological studies of the plays were also intriguing; all those absurd theories of the human mind. "Freud was a fool," I thought. "But a fascinating fool." For a moment I could imagine spending my entire life expanding on his theories, creating a fictional map of the human soul based as much on my own idiosyncrasies as on any generalized human being.

At last, my eyes grew tired and weak, my body cramped, dizzy with sitting in one place, my mind clouded and confused with mazes of theories that crossed and intersected but seemed to lead only to dead ends. I burst out into the garden, out of the dust, filling my lungs with fresh air. "Angel!" I cried. "Angel or Devil! Where are you? I'm ready. I'm ready!" But only silence met me. I rushed over to a huge pomegranate tree and shook it violently, though it just stood like a massive stone. "Angel," I cried again and again, descending into a soft whimper. I stood awhile, hugging the tree like a scorned lover, then reached up and grabbed an enormous pomegranate. Peeling its rind, I sucked its sweet fruits slowly, one by one, spitting the seeds carelessly upon the ground. As I ate, I sank lower and lower into the shadow of the tree, into the roots. "What a piece of work is man," echoed in my brain, "how noble in reason, how infinite in faculty, in form and moving how express and admirable, in action how like an angel . . . ."

I awoke in blackness, unable to see the tree. Confused, I arose and wandered, as if by instinct, back to the library where the single lamp remained shining, *Shakespeare's Complete Works* lying discarded beside the chair. I realized I had better study it some more to be prepared when the angel returned. The lamp was even dimmer, like it might flicker out, just enough light to illuminate Shakespeare's ancient words, and I made my way through his plays one final time. At first, the words appeared distant, but as I read through the dizzy night they touched my brain with a new sensation. They began to seem full of vigor, more than mere words. They wove together, a great tapestry. A map began to form in my mind, as Shakespeare's characters took on a new poignancy. I felt their innermost thoughts, felt as though I actually were them, banished and sailing across the ocean, or winning and losing great battles, or plotting revenge upon a tyrant, or losing my greatest love, or marrying happily ever after, or swallowing poison to end this bitter life. A map of the human soul. I could feel the neurons in my brain weaving together, creating new paths of meaning, each little neuron corresponding to a word, yet far more than a word, humming and vibrating. I stood with Lear alone on the heath, wind howling, blind and mad, crowned with weeds and flowers. I could stand it no more and hurled the cursed volume across the room. Then I ran outside. It was coal black, but I had read so long that it must have been the next night's darkness, or perhaps the next month's. The dark enveloped me, swallowed me, so I was unable to locate even my own emotions. I squirmed underneath what I thought was the pomegranate tree and, still wandering with Lear upon the heath, fell into nothingness.

I awoke to a huge light, a cathedral with vast stained-glass windows, pictures of chess pieces, cards, monopoly boards, and games beyond counting, light in rainbow colors streaming through, filling the huge nave. I was lying on a bench beside a stone table. The angel hovered over me, wings beating like a hummingbird. Although rather dizzy, I managed to raise myself to a seated position. "I'm ready for the test," I said. "Or at least as ready as I'll ever be. What is it? Multiple choice? Essay? Whatever. I can't swear I'll pass it, but I'll do my best."

"You have already passed," she said, her voice resonating like an overly large cow bell, "although in a way that is little better than failure."

I was overjoyed, but not for long enough to take even one breath. The angel informed that we were in the Temple of Games, that the next task was a light one, an interlude. I was to pick a game, to test my skill against the angel's. I thought a bit, then selected backgammon.

"A lot of luck in that one," she said. "It'll have to be two out of three."

We played on an ornate board, silver-white and heavy gold inlaid with sparkling rubies, a board so enormous I had, at times, to walk across it to move my pieces, though the angel dispensed her moves with a flick of the wrist. Her pieces were shaped like famous monarchs and world conquerors—Queen Victoria, Julius Caesar, Alexander the Great—mine like court jesters, toadies, and comics from Hollywood B movies. The first game went badly; she had me trapped, two of my pieces knocked out. It appeared hopeless for me, but the dice rolled in such a way that she had to leave a hole in her setup. If I rolled double fours, I'd not only get back on the board, but knock off one of her pieces, a stern likeness of Winston Churchill. I rubbed the dice, blew on them and silently prayed to some higher power (though lord help me if that higher power turned out to be the angel herself). Strangely enough— though utterly predictably, in hindsight—up came two fours. Gleefully, my pieces rounded the board while hers remained trapped. I rolled doubles several times more that game and won handily.

The second game, unsurprisingly, was a disaster. She was down to one final piece while I had removed nothing; it would be a double game, the series would be over, and I would have lost, unworthy of moving on to my final tasks. Why, oh why, had I chosen to cast my fate to mere luck?

I cast the dice—double sixes! Jerry Lewis gleefully rounded the board, and out. It was tied, one to one.

The third game was wild. We each played boldly, recklessly leaving pieces open, taking great risks to gain an advantage, hitting each others' pieces with abandon. Neither could form a potent bloc; we remained scattered and diffuse. At one point she had five pieces knocked out; at another I had six. Finally, I began a spectacular series of rolls that led me to a guaranteed victory. What was more, double fours (that number again!) would give me a double game. I rolled and, shockingly, there they were—no more and no less. I had beat her three games to one.

"I knew I should have insisted on chess," she said miserably.

"I'm great at that, too," I said, although deep down I knew that, when ahead, I tended to make mistakes and end up losing. "In fact, I had no trouble passing any of your tests. I even wish I hadn't refused that one about ending poverty on Earth."

"The rules say that I can't give you the same one you've already refused. But I've a similar one for you—to bring about peace on Earth. Good will toward men—and women—optional."

"Wait," I gasped, but before I could explain I was only joking, I found myself in the mountains among a tribe of goat herders, whom I soon learned were called the Urks. They were Asiatic in appearance, skin not quite yellow, not quite brown, with piercing eyes. Their tools were primitive but sturdy: solid staffs, well-crafted pottery, lavishly ornamented religious implements. The only modern thing about them was their weapons, slung behind their backs, assault rifles whose snouts grinned evilly at the sky. Oddly enough, I found I spoke their language and asked why they were so heavily armed. It turned out they were battling an enemy tribe who was supplied with modern weapons from "evil socialist foreigners."

I lived awhile among these people, who shared everything, who seemed to know little greed. They herded sheep in the day and sang jangly songs on stringed instruments at night, wailing in a piercing sing-song, telling stories of doomed love and their tribe's long history. It seemed idyllic, except for their constant vigilance against enemy raids.

If I was to be a peacemaker, I realized I'd better get to know the enemy tribe, the Skri. I hated this tribe, for I had heard of their treachery, of how they had negotiated for peace then massacred the Urks, of how they raped women, tortured men, and tossed babies from rooftops. When I reached them, however, they seemed more advanced, at least technologically, than the Urks. They were a trading people with widespread outposts, as well as fine artisans weaving fabulous murals that told of ancient myths. They were also great traders and merchants, especially fond of jewels, and loving to amass wealth. Indeed, they were more bloodthirsty than the Urks, with long feuds over money and women that would erupt into sporadic violence. They also poached the dwindling elephant herds; I saw them kill a great beast once, stripping its flesh, greedily seizing its tusks. Though the Skri had admirable qualities, the Urks were right to hate them, I thought secretly, for soon there would be no elephants, yet the Skri were heedless. They complained bitterly of the evil, faraway "capitalist imperialists" who supplied the Urks with modern weapons.

Now my negotiating began. Using my status as an outsider, tall and white yet familiar with both tribes' languages, I suggested a peace gathering. The Council of the Urks balked, remembering earlier massacres, yet I assured them that, if the negotiators from both sides laid down their weapons, and each could inspect the other, all would go well. I personally swore to oversee both sides, to check on their compliance. Finally, both sides agreed. Perhaps peace was at hand?

I was heady with success. Wandering across the mountain ranges to the site of the negotiations, which quickly coalesced into a peace treaty, I felt myself to be a great ambassador. I had succeeded with the Urks and Skri. A long, arduous journey lay ahead, bringing peace to the world, but I felt ready, almost superhuman. It would be a sort of snowball effect, an accelerating momentum, gathering force, peace feeding upon peace as I negotiated in country after country, applying reason, logic, calmness, bringing warring parties together as they realized the futility of war. Country after country would join in a great onrush of peace! Emotion swelled within me, I could feel hot tears, stinging my cheeks with salt, at the thought of so much human generosity. And me at the helm! It would take years, perhaps my whole life. But after all, if Alexander the Great could, through war, reach the distant gates of India by the time he was thirty, I could bring about world peace before I turned seventy. Or perhaps a little after.

A sound like popcorn popping. Bloody figures appeared wailing before me. I had reached the site of the peace treaty only to be surrounded by death. Bodies lay sprawled before me, gushing pure redness, more red than I could have believed existed, blood blood blood blood blood, red red red red red.

In the distance, sporadic gunfire. I dashed toward the chaos of bodies, knelt, dipped my hands in the blood of one young woman as it pulsed outward. Around me, in all directions, the flags and uniforms of the Skri. "Oh God," I cried out. "What have I done!" I was bathed in blood. Limbs and heads riddled with bullets. Every pathway covered in blood. I bounded toward the gunfire, which grew more distant, chased with huge bounds, felt myself as a jackrabbit or grasshopper, till my feet ceased touching the ground. Finally, I reached a small body of Skri holding out against the attacking Urks. I threw myself in front of them and the Urks ceased fire, allowing the Skri to escape.

Standing before the vengeful Urks, "What have you done?" I cried.

"We had to," said the tallest of the Urks, glaring at me with piercing, confident eyes, "or they would have done the same to us. You don't know the Skri."

"The peace treaty. It was genius. I'd worked out everything. Every detail."

"They would have found a way to break it. You don't know the Skri."

I bowed down and wept. "I've failed," I said. "What a fool I've been."

I lay prostrate, sobbing great gasping sobs that grew in intensity, each gasp sucking in a larger and larger volume of air till my lungs were ready to burst. The sheer volume choked me—I couldn't believe there was that much air in all the universe, yet I kept sucking, gasping.

Overhead, a vast figure loomed: the angel.

"I have one more task for you," she said, in a voice that seemed an echo of itself, a voice both inside and outside myself.

"It's too late. I've failed at the most important task, the only one that really mattered."

"We're more easygoing than that where I come from," she said, suddenly shrunk to normal size. "we allow four out of five tasks. That's eighty percent. A B minus."

She insisted I sleep before she announced my final task. When I awoke, as if to a world utterly new, she gave me an extraordinarily strong cappuccino in a tiny cup. It singed my fingers, but I swallowed the drink, lingered awhile, then asked for my final task, which she calmly announced:

"To leave your one true love."

"No," I gasped. "Anything but that."

"We pick the tasks. You have no say."

"Why not? Who are you, anyway? Why do you keep tormenting me so? What power do you have over me?"

At this the angel broke down and wept, a great flood of tears like rain from the heavens. "You don't know what a terrible position we supernatural beings are in. We must seem cruel and capricious to you. Believe me, there's a purpose to all of this." We were on a small raft and her tears formed a rising tide lifting us toward the dazzling sun, a rainbow of purples and crimsons in the water below. Oblivious, she continued sobbing until her face was twisted and wretched, reminding me of my one true love at her lowest point, of how I'd comforted here.

I reached out to the angel and hugged her. "Don't worry angel," I said. "I'll do what you say."

At this, her very touch stung me, and I leapt backwards, falling off the raft. "Wonderful," she said, her face a hideous grin, as I swam in the ocean of tears, desperately struggling to grab onto the heaving vessel.

Then I thought of my one true love, her hair black as midnight, her warm brown eyes, how she comforted me when I was unhappy, tended to me when I was ill, how at this very moment she was bearing my first child. "I can't do it," I said.

"Too late," answered the angel with an insipid giggle. "We already have a verbal commitment. Can't go back on that." She disappeared and I found myself back on earth, sure I hadn't dreamt the thing, not one word or sensation of it.

Since that time, my true love has left me. Indeed, I found out she was sleeping with another man all along. And now she has borne a child—his or mine, I can't say. I have a premonition, though, that this child will be tormented by the same angel when she grows up. My only comfort is in knowing that I passed the angel's tests. A B minus.

At night, I think of my true love, imagine her warm touch, her soft voice murmuring like a peaceful brook I played in when I was small. I was certain that brook would always be there. Now it's gone and so is she. I feel a great betrayal. And somehow, I am sure the angel is behind it. Perhaps I did fail her tests. And at night I can't sleep. I lie there pondering, what could I have done differently. Was the fault in me or in the five impossible tasks? In the distance, I seem to hear the angel cackling, gleefully and without pity.

The Realm of Wake and the Realm of Sleep

Eons ago, when humanity had just emerged from the womb of a rather pretentious ape, there were two realms: the Realm of Wake and the Realm of Sleep. Humans dwelt exclusively in the land of wake, hunting and fishing, gathering roots and berries day after day after day. During the long nights, humans solved logic problems to prepare for the technological future that is our destiny, the pinnacle of our success and glory that will bring about our extinction along with a million species.

In that dawn era, other beings dwelt in the land of sleep, not quite shadow creatures, human yet not human. Unencumbered by the laws of physics, they flitted about in a surreal multiscape where time and space were fluid, altered partly through individual whim, partly through group desire, partly through a mysterious third force unnamed to this day (though some may call it god, spiritual essence, dark matter, or quantum mechanics). These dream humans created language, told stories, wrote poetry, sang songs, painted shifting landscapes, sculpted creatures that came alive, performed plays, all with no progression or logic, no theme rising to a climax. In these proto-arts, events, sounds, and feelings were strewn about at random, ghouls, eerie noises, sewage smells, and weeping fallen angels appearing alongside roses, dandelions, Venus fly traps, elephants, cherubs, and soaring hymns. Morality was never judged and the same being could easily do good one moment and harm the next. Identity could alter from instant to instant and time itself could easily flow backward or sideways, dripping away into space or returning as a fifth, sixth, or seventeenth dimension.

One day a human, tired of the Realm of Wake and curious about what lay beyond, undertook an epic journey across a treacherous landscape and then, in a small boat, over a tempestuous sea, to find the Realm of Sleep. Meanwhile, as if a twin, a being from the Realm of

Sleep undertook a reverse journey across abstract floating landscapes filled with ever-shifting impressions and found herself encumbered, as she approached the outermost edge of the Realm of Wake, by the need to take physical steps, increasingly heavy. More and more, the slowing crawl of time dripped upon her like some preternatural superglue. All previous incursions from the Realm of Sleep had been quickly abandoned because, after all, who would choose to be bound by the laws of space and time? For an inexplicable reason, some quirk of will, this being did not turn back, perhaps intrigued by the realization that challenges can be overcome with individual determination, that she could build something called character, a quality not experienced in the Realm of Sleep.

Some call the first human from the Land of Wake brave enough to approach the Realm of Sleep Adam and the woman crossing the border of that distant land Eve. Feminists decry this, claiming it reduces women to lesser beings, shadowy, amoral, lacking rationality. Some militant feminists challenge the first group of feminists, claiming the Realm of Sleep as superior, as that which generates creativity, just as only women can bear children, the ultimate creative act. In any case, the story of Adam and Eve is reductive, as are all attempts to make the story of humanity understandable, to contain form and meaning. In a sense, even writing these words is futile, as is poring over *the Bible*, the *Koran*, or the *Bhagavad Gita*.

Reader, you know the rest and experience it every day. It is your life, the surreal creative and the rational bound together in one body, one variegated mind, more powerful together than chocolate and peanut butter, yet more ephemeral. It is your gift and your curse.